Dedicated to Nika, Cheuk, Toby and Tilly

Boggarts, Trolls & Tylwyth Teg

Peter Stevenson

The History Press

First published 2021
Reprinted 2023

The History Press
97 St George's Place,
Cheltenham GL50 3QB
www.thehistorypress.co.uk

British Library Cataloguing in Publication Data.
A catalogue record for this book is available from the British Library.

ISBN 978 0 7509 9562 7

Typesetting and origination by The History Press
Printed by TJ Books Limited, Padstow, Cornwall

'There's no identity problem,
only a problem of identity.'

*Tony Hopkins, black Cherokee storyteller,
actor and poet from New Zealand*

Contents

Foreword

What a delight it was to have Welsh storyteller and friend Peter Stevenson visit our local *marae* to share Welsh stories alongside my partners' African and Native American tales and myths and legends from my own land *Aotearoa/New Zealand*.

Although our stories came from different hemispheres and cultures, we recognised in each other's tales the familiar characters of the trickster, the fairy folk and those wise, wily or sometimes frightening mythical creatures such as our *Aotearoa taniwha*. We found that by sharing our different stories we were not only entertained but we also were connected.

For me as a *Pākehā* New Zealander (a person descended from New Zealand settlers, many of whom were English, Welsh, Irish and Scottish), hearing Peter tell traditional stories using Welsh phrases and words that some of my ancestors would have recognised was both moving and thought provoking.

The fact that the indigenous people of Wales and *Aotearoa* were persecuted for speaking their own language, practising their cultural traditions and telling their own stories gives both cultures a shared experience. Today, as people of many cultures work to ensure their languages and traditions survive in an ever-changing world, storytellers such as Peter Stevenson ensure the stories will also survive. In this, they do us all a great service and are truly *taonga* (something precious).

Moira Wairama

Introduction

As a scruffy child, I liked clambering over the remains of the 150 iron-age stone roundhouses in the Giants' Town on the summit of Tre'r Ceiri on Pen Llŷn in north-west Wales, because from there I could see the whole wide world. Well, maybe not all of it, but the Wicklow Hills 60 kilometres to the west in Poblacht na hÉireann, the mountains of the English Lake District in the faraway north and the island of Ellan Vannin in the Irish Sea. And out there in Cardigan Bay were two mythical lands, the submerged city of Cantre'r Gwaelod that illuminated the sea with the setting sun, and the utopian land of Plant Rhys Ddwfn, the Children of Rhys the Deep, a folk philosopher's dream of a better world (read the full story in The Epilogue p.213).

However, all these mystical lands were usually hidden by what my mam called 'The Steam', or more poetically, '*Y Brenin Llwyd*' (the Grey King), a thick mist that sits on top of Tre'r Ceiri and prevents anyone seeing beyond the ends of their noses. Undaunted, I learned that if I squinted and used my imagination, I could see a town full of hidden giants, several faraway countries, a lost submerged land and a forgotten utopia, and all were equally real in my childhood mythology.

Below Tre'r Ceiri is the mountain village of Llithfaen, where three generations ago the older folk told tales in Welsh as *chwedlau*, a weaving together of myth, conversation and gossip. They left the village every Wednesday, packed like sardines onto Glyn's old Leyland Tiger bus that rattled along the single-track road to the Wednesday market in Pwllheli. What it lacked in suspension it made up for in stories and chickens. After the granite quarry closed in 1964, the stoneworkers' houses in Nant Gwrtheyrn fell derelict and were squatted by hippies who knew little of the stories of the land. The coastal villages were becoming retirement homes and holiday camps, house prices were rising, and young people were leaving for jobs in cities over the border. People were vanishing.

The giants watched from the mountain as Carl Clowes, the local doctor, founded Antur Aelhaearn, the first community co-operative in the UK, and gave me my first job on leaving college, painting designs on the pottery and firing the kiln of an evening. The deserted village of Nant Gwrtheyrn was renovated and transformed into the National Welsh Language Centre. The land was reborn, Rhys Ddwfn's utopian dreams had come true, and I learned that people could be giants, too. Myths and real life were intricately intertwined.

Back in the late 1800s, Griffith Griffith, a chapel man from Edern, was crossing the heather below Tre-r Ceiri, when he saw a crowd of little men and women walking towards him, speaking a language he didn't understand. He wasn't afraid, so he stood by the ditch to let them pass. He didn't know where they were from, so he called them '*Tylwyth teg*' – fairies.

Elis Bach, a farmer's son from Tŷ Canol in Nant Gwrtheyrn, was thought to be a changeling child, because his legs were so short his body almost touched the ground. One day, he and his dog Meg saw some men herding stolen sheep up the corkscrew road. He jumped out on them, did a weird dance, and chased them off. Elis was no supernatural creature; he was born in the village and spoke Welsh. He was Tylwyth teg because he was different, like those visitors who treated Welsh speakers as if they were from another planet.

Time passed, and I became a book illustrator and storyteller, and these skills allowed me to meet people from cultures across the world and hear tales of their lives and lands. One such encounter led to the writing of this book. For thirty years I've worked with the New Zealand publisher, Sunshine Books of Auckland, illustrating stories by great children's writers like Joy Cowley and Margaret Mahy. Although a stranger back then, my visual storytelling has now become a small part of the lives of two or three generations of *Pākehā*, Māori, *Pasifika* and Chinese children.

At Christmas 2019, my friend Moira Wairama, *Pākehā* storyteller and writer, invited me and my son to her local *marae* in Stokes Valley where I was to tell tales of the Tylwyth teg. Moira introduced me to stories of the Patupaiarehe, the little people of the Aotearoa bush, while her partner, storyteller and actor Tony Hopkins, is rooted in the storytelling tradition of the Yunwi tsunsdi, the Cherokee little people.

While Patupaiarehe, Yunwi tsunsdi and Tylwyth teg may appear to be sisters from three separate continents, they each grew from their own landscapes and cultures, spoke their native tongues, and travelled in the darker margins of our minds to meet in New Zealand as stories.

A *tangi*, a Māori funeral, was taking place next door, so we paid our respects to the bereaved family who sat on cushions around an open casket surrounded by the painted and carved wooden walls that depicted the myths of the Stokes Valley *iwi*. We were introduced with spontaneous stories and songs in a moment of shared community and mythology that celebrated death within life. This was the root and branch of visual storytelling; a moment of transition no international zoom event could ever replicate. And I understood what it was like to be Tylwyth teg – from the Otherworld (read more in the chapter Patupaiarehe).

In mythology, lost lands are coral castles beneath the sea where mermaids swim, ancient forests where spirits live among the trees, mountain swamps where trolls lurk, thinly veiled dimensions haunted by ghosts, underground hell worlds full of demons, and darkness where fairies fly on gossamer wings. Strip away the mythology, and lost lands become valleys and villages flooded to provide drinking water to neighbouring kingdoms, inner cities where people exist on fairy money, closed doors that conceal tales of domestic abuse and mental health, campsites where travellers are told they can't travel, migrants displaced by war and hunger, and reservations where the rights of First Nations people are ignored.

Stories of encounters with those from the otherworld are about Them and Us, and ask simple questions, 'Are you scary or friendly? Do you speak our language? Should we welcome you or build a wall and keep you away?' Look into a face, and we make assumptions about gender and race, but only when we hear their stories do the walls between us tumble down. No flimsy border can stop a good story from crossing over, rooting itself and growing leaves in its new home. African mermaids, Chinese fox fairies and Indian weretigers all flourish in Wales.

An international approach to folktales through collaborations, permissions and acknowledgements helps understand the nature of 'otherness'. Yet there must be sensitivity to appropriation, for folktales are a living reflection of their own cultures, people and landscape, and a story torn from its context is merely a text. Yet it's important to find ways to surmount what Bong Joon Ho, director of the South Korean film *Parasite*, called 'the one-inch-tall barrier of subtitles'.

The tales in this book have grown from conversations with storytellers, writers, artists, academics, historians, educationalists, friends and family across the world, encountered on my travels and in my small multicultural Welsh hometown. In the tradition of storytelling, that delicate balance between art and academia, I tell the stories in my own words while keeping close to the emotional and physical landscapes of the tellers who are themselves woven into the chapters. And a very special thanks to my dear friend Veronika Derkova for reading through the manuscript and for the countless inspiring conversations in her bee garden.

In my mythology, all stories begin in West Wales, so this tour of lost lands and hidden people starts with a changeling child who may have been a famous poet, followed by a Scottish selkie who came from the sea to save an old fisherman, the Korrigan who stopped a Breton stonewaller building across their unseen land, the Irish hidden people who prevented the felling of fairy hawthorns, Scandinavian trolls from a misunderstood native culture, a poor bewitched camel infatuated with a wealthy Syrian princess, a Mauritian hare who took whatever he wanted like colonialists before him, the huli jing from the invisible male dreamworld of old China, the Gullah people of North Carolina and West Africa who knew how to fly, the Duwamish of Seattle who officially don't exist, and back to the utopia of West Wales to meet Morwen, the mermaid who inspired a renowned writer in the western world.

Oh, and not forgetting the nasty Jezinka girls from the Czech Republic who steal people's eyes so they can't see what's in front of their noses, just like the mist on the Welsh mountains.

1

The Crow and the Canary: Part One

CYMRU, WALES

Three years ago, the Welsh Government's tourism department designated 2017 as *Flwyddyn Chwedlau Cymru*, the Year of Legends. Wales was given a makeover as a mythological land where King Arthur strode like a giant, magicians mixed potions in cauldrons on mountaintops, mermaids swam through plastic-free seas, and impoverished storytellers were offered unexpected employment. However, hidden behind the marketing was another storytelling tradition that mixed legends with local gossip, spontaneous wit and contemporary injustices.

In this looking-glass world, mystical ladies who lived beneath lakes were replaced by people displaced from villages flooded to build reservoirs to supply drinking water to cities over the border. And these tales of lost lands and hidden people were told in the native Welsh language, spoken by people and mermaids alike.

This story begins with a translation of a Welsh-language fairy tale from the writer, illustrator, and educator Myra Evans, from Ceinewydd, on the coast of Ceredigion, and is followed by a mostly true tale pieced together from conversations with her daughter, Iola Billings, and many walks in the shared landscape of both tales. Myra's archive is the richest collection of oral folk tales in Wales, yet she is barely remembered as a footnote in the life of an internationally famous poet who lived his life as the hero of one of her stories.

A woman was wandering, lost and lovelorn, in the Llwynwermwnt woods near Ceinewydd, when she sensed someone behind her. She turned and there was a man, hair in golden ringlets, eyes green as spring pools, and a smile of pearly white milk teeth. He kissed her

hand, held her round the waist and laid her down on the mossy ground. When she came to, he had done as all creepy men who lurk in the woods in fairy tales always do. He'd vanished.

All that day she searched for him and all the following day, all that week and the following week, and all that month till nine months passed, when she gave birth to a beautiful baby boy, curling gold hair, spring green eyes, and pearly white milk teeth. Her anger for the man who had abused her melted into love for her fairy child.

The woman lived at the Llwynwermwnt Farmhouse outside Ceinewydd. She sang as sweetly as a canary, but her husband was a simple, stolid man who croaked like a crow. He knew the names of all his sheep, but not the name of the child he assumed was his.

Late one afternoon, the woman was feeding her baby when her pap ran dry, so she took a jug and went outside to milk the cow. It mooed agitatedly and kicked at the pail. As she returned to the farmhouse, she noticed the door was ajar and she thought she'd closed it. The fire blazed in the hearth, and she knew she'd dampened it down. Her baby sat upright in his wooden cradle, gnashing and grinding his teeth, gurning his face into weird contortions and staring with eyes the colour of autumn, his golden locks turned ash brown.

She wrapped him up warm in his cradle and ran down the hill to an old ramshackle cottage overlooking the sea at Banc Penrhiw, encircled by enchanter's nightshade and wild garlic. She knocked on the oak door and there stood old Beti Grwca, a thousand wrinkles around her eyes, a single grey hair in the middle of her chin, and a solitary yellow tooth that wobbled unnervingly in the breeze from her breath.

'*Dewch i mewn, cariad,*' old Beti ushered her in. '*Bara brith? Paned?*'

The ochre walls were lined with sagging shelves filled with green and brown bottles. Beti laid the table with fruit bread and a pot of thin Tregaron tea.

'Help yourself, and don't mind the cat and her little ways. Now what can I do?'

As the woman explained, old Beti wrinkled her eyes and pulled on the one grey hair in the middle of her chin and said, '*Cariad*, this may not be your babi. It may be an *anwadalyn*, a changeling child, left by the otherworld!'

Beti shuffled over to the dresser, took a large duck egg, pricked both ends, blew out the contents, and stuffed it with bread, cheese and milk.

'In the morning, break this egg onto seven plates, make sure your babi is watching, say nothing, do nothing, come and tell me what you hear and see.'

The woman took the egg and walked home over the hill with her moonlit shadow following behind. The cow mooed agitatedly in the farmyard, the door was ajar, and she was sure she'd closed it, the fire blazed in the hearth, and she knew she'd dampened it down. Her baby spat into the fire and stared through wide autumn eyes with the knowledge of a thousand and a half years. Dark thoughts danced in her head. If this was an *anwadalyn*, should she drown it in the deep dank pond at Nantypele farm?

In the morning she laid the table with seven plates, broke open the egg, and a feast of bread, cheese and milk filled the table. Brown eyes followed her round the kitchen as she stoked the fire, stared into the flames, and listened:

Mesen welais cyn gweld derwen
Gwelais wy cyn gweled cyw
Ond ni welais fwyd i fedel
Mewn un plisgyn yn fy myw

['I saw an acorn before an oak, I saw an egg before a chick, but I never saw food from one shell.']

The woman ran to old Beti, who wrinkled her eyes, pulled on the one grey hair in the middle of her chin, and said, '*Cariad*, this is an *anwadalyn*. Come with me, say nothing, do as I say.'

Beti took the woman's hand and they followed their shadows over the hill to the Llwynwermwnt farmhouse. The cow was hysterical, the door banged on its hinges, the fire blazed in the hearth, and the baby sat upright in its cradle. It ground and gnashed its teeth and it's bulging brown eyes stared straight into their souls.

Beti snatched it up, ignored the screams and curses, and scurried over the hill to the Nantypele farm pond as it gnawed her shoulder. She thrust it into the woman's arms and told her to hurl it into the dank depths. The woman stared into its bloodshot autumn eyes, and in that moment, she knew this was not her baby. She hurled it with all her strength, and as it screamed through the air and hit the surface, the waters boiled and the Tylwyth teg appeared, dressed in red rags and with shaggy red hair, and they dragged their wayward child into the depths, leaving a clinging coldness in the air.

Old Beti led the woman by the hand back to Llwynwermwnt. The cow was contentedly chewing the cud, the door was carefully latched, the fire dampened in the hearth, and there gurgling in his cradle was her golden-haired baby. She held him to her breast and kissed him, and never noticed that while one eye was green as the spring, the other was still brown as autumn.

Myra Evans was born in 1883 in Ceinewydd, not far from the Llwynwermwnt farmhouse, at midnight between All Souls and *Calan Gaeaf*, the first day of winter in the Welsh calendar, when the veil between this world and the other is at its thinnest and those from the otherworld pass through and make mischief. Myra stared at the world through her brown eyes of autumn and grew into an inquisitive girl who loved to dress up as a mourner and attend funerals, once in a red dress amongst the crow black, always walking a tightrope between her two worlds. She loved to sing, but she squawked like an old crow.

Her father Thomas was a fisherman, captain of the *Rosina*, who had lost all his five brothers at sea. Myra was his fish-girl. She sat beside him on the pier gutting the herring and mackerel while he told her fairy tales learned from the old sea captains of the town. She wrote down his stories and kept them in a biscuit tin under her bed to read while he was away at sea. Here were stories of red-haired mermaids, vanishing harpers and fleet-footed fairy fiddlers, characters from the West Welsh Otherworld familiar to everyone 100 years ago, a charmed state where time passed in the blink of a crow's eye or the length of an endless final heartbeat, where you could vanish as easily as a language. There were few kings and princesses in Myra's world.

Myra married her childhood sweetheart, Evan Jenkin Evans, a nuclear physicist from Llanelli who studied in Manchester with Ernest Rutherford. Their firstborn David died young, while the second, Aneurin, grew into a mischievous child, who climbed out of his bedroom window in Chorlton when he was 3 and was found eating an ice cream in a city-centre cinema by the Manchester Police, who couldn't understand a word he said as he spoke only Welsh.

In the early 1920s, Evan was offered work in the Physics Department at the fledgling Swansea University, so the family moved to suburban Sketty, with its semi-detached villas and stained-glass windows, where people spoke posh. Sex sounded like the sacks that coal was delivered in.

Myra taught Welsh in the Swansea schools when the language was discouraged by the authorities, she wrote and illustrated the first Welsh language primer and persuaded Foyle's of London to publish it, she worked for the BBC telling nature stories in Welsh on the radio, and she published a small collection of her father's fairy tales, *Casgliad o Chwedlau Newydd*, to raise money for the restoration of the Tabernacl Chapel roof in Ceinewydd. One of those tales was the 'Anwadalyn Llwynwermwnt'.

Aneurin went to Swansea Grammar School with the mischievous son of Myra's neighbours in Sketty, David and Florence Thomas. David, an English teacher at the school, loved Welsh mythology yet taught his son in English, while Myra spoke to her boy in his native language.

The young Thomas was molly-coddled by his mam, stole sweets, fell out of trees, broke bones and was as cheeky as any changeling child. He had a head full of golden curls, eyes of autumn brown, and they named him Dylan.

Dylan had all the disadvantages of a happy childhood. He decided to be a poet, a hard-living bohemian looked after by rich crows – soft, silly ravens, he called them. He had all the qualifications. He was an outsider who wrote about himself, rather than the romance of the Welsh landscape.

By 1934, Dylan had lost his jobs at the local newspaper and the Swansea Little Theatre, his first book of poetry had been accepted by a London publisher, and he had a girlfriend in Battersea. He left the comforting arms of the Mumbles Mermaid and crossed the border into the neighbouring kingdom, where he slayed the giants of the London literary world and charmed the dragon, Dame Edith Sitwell, who favourably reviewed his book.

He attended the court of King John, the painter Augustus, where he met the golden-haired Princess Caitlin and wooed her with words, not swords. He was left lying in a car park in Carmarthen after the king found him in a compromising position with the princess on the back seat of his car. He spent the summer of 1935 in a remote cottage in Donegal, writing, walking, fishing, running up debts, insulting the locals and trying to dry out. He was joined for a fortnight by Geoffrey Grigson, then editor of *New Verse* magazine, who referred to him as 'The Swansea Changeling', left by the Otherworld under a foxglove.

In September 1944, the changeling child, his golden-haired princess and their two young children left the land of falling bombs for the wild West Welsh coast, and by one of those curious coincidences you only find in fairy tales, in the same month of the same year, Myra Evans and her mischievous son and youngest daughter moved into a blue bungalow down the lane.

The story continues in 'The Crow and the Canary, Part Two' on page 207.

2

The Silkie Painter

I first heard this story forty-odd years ago as a post-grad at Leeds University's Institute of Dialect and Folklife Studies, which was hidden away in the basement of a terraced house, at least until its closure in 1984. I had completed my art degree, and had transformed into an academic folklorist, and this new skin was itchy. The head of the institute, Stewart Sanderson, had been the archivist at the School of Scottish Studies in Edinburgh, and he introduced me to the story of the selkie artist, a tale of split identity and misunderstood people, which in that moment spoke volumes to me. The storyteller was the legendary Scottish traveller, Duncan Williamson.

Duncan was born in 1928 in a traveller camp in Argyll, one of sixteen children to parents who couldn't read and a people who were cruelly persecuted and vilified. He went to school but left aged 13 to work as a stonemason, horse dealer, drystone dyker, farmhand, once as a boxing instructor, and for thirty days as an inmate in Perth Prison for breaking a man's jaw. He jumped the broomstick with his first wife Jeannie when she was 16, and they had seven children, but these are mere facts.

Duncan famously said, 'Never let the truth stand in the way of a good story', and he also told storytellers to look over their shoulders at the person who told them the tale, for behind them would be all the previous tellers. I learned to always acknowledge sources, as academics are trained to do. Though I never got the hang of footnotes.

Duncan disapproved of excess academia, at least until he married the folklorist and musicologist Linda Headlee from the School of Scottish Studies, who arrived one day to interview him. She encouraged him to write down and publish his stories and contact the storytelling festival world. So, his tales of cheeky Jack and the fairies turned him into a man of two worlds.

He published *Tales of the Seal People* in 1992, a collection of silkie stories pieced together from tales he knew from the traveller community. By then, I'd shed my academic skin and returned to the world of illustration and books. And almost thirty years later, maybe Scotland is preparing to tear off the skin of a disunited kingdom and swim free as a silkie.

In a stone cottage on the west coast of Scotland lived two old fisherfolk, John and Mary, who farmed the sea, salted and dried the herring, and sold them at the Wednesday market. On warm evenings, they sat on the shingle outside their front door and mended the nets after the seals had bitten holes in them to eat the fish inside. John hated the seals.

'Those seals are taking my living,' he said, 'There'll be no food on the table, and what will we do then? They should all be shot, those seals.'

'Oh, don't make a fuss,' said Mary, 'the sea provides food enough for us all.'

Well, the old fisherman grumbled as Mary shooed him indoors, sat him down at the kitchen table and placed a bowl of fish soup in front of him. He splashed it down his sweater in between mouthfuls, while he complained it might be his last meal, thanks to those seals.

One day, Mary had filled her leather apron with dulse, red seaweed that she dried and sold at the market, when she spotted a shape on the shoreline. She hurried towards it, thinking it might be a body, only to find a seal pup staring up at her with big saucery eyes. She looked around for its parents, for grown seals can be fearsome creatures when they have a baby, but there were none to be seen. 'Poor little orphan,' she thought, as she wrapped it in her apron with the dulse, hurried back to the cottage, and laid it in the old wooden cradle John had carved before her miscarriage. She covered it in the red patchwork quilt from their bed, fed it a small mackerel, and listened as the wind rattled the loose panes.

When the old fisherman came home, he was still grumbling about the holes in his nets, when he saw the seal pup.

'What's that doing here? In my cradle! Wrapped in my quilt. Eating my fish. Where's my gun?' he blustered.

Mary had hidden the gun in the woodshed.

'Now calm yourself, John,' she said. 'It has no parents, and it would have died on the beach if I hadn't brought it home.'

'Well, let it die,' he grumbled, 'or it will have babies, and they will eat all my fish, too.' And he spat into the fire.

'Calm down,' she said. 'They aren't all your fish, they are to be shared.'

That evening, the old man gnashed his teeth and swore he would kill every seal in the sea. They were preparing for bed when there was a knock on the door.

John said, 'Don't answer. It might be the bailiffs come to evict us and ship us to America.'

Mary told him not to be foolish and she opened the door to a tall young man with dark curling hair, thick on top and short at the sides, a long nose and high cheekbones. He wore a navy fisherman's jumper with a knitting pattern unique to his home port and an initial embroidered into the hem, to identify his body if it washed up on shore. John didn't recognise the pattern.

The young man apologised for calling so late, but he was looking for lodgings in the town and there were no beds to be had. The landlord suggested asking here. He only needed a small room, as he would be out all day and gone inside a week. He was a painter, intent on capturing the landscape of the seashore on canvas. He would be no trouble at all. His name was Iain.

Mary said they would rent him a room, and John added they were short of money because those pesky seals were eating all his profits. Mary elbowed him under the ribs, and they led Iain upstairs to a bedroom.

'This is our room,' whispered John, 'where will we sleep?'

Mary replied, 'In the child's room. Hush now.'

Iain declared the room perfect and assured them he would not make a mess. He only had a portable easel, some canvases, a sketchbook and a water jug for rinsing his brushes, and he mostly worked outdoors as he drew from life. He gave them a week's rent, and hands were shaken. Mary said Iain must help himself to porridge and herring for breakfast, and he could join them for an evening meal. The old man told him not to help himself to all the fish, though, as those sea …'

Mary elbowed him again and he stifled the pain. And she couldn't help but repeat Iain's name to herself.

The following day, Iain was up and out early, and returned in the evening at the same time as John. They had fish and tatties, and lit a fire, and Iain told them tales of the mischievous *sidhe* and *broonies* from MacGregor's *The Peat-Fire Flame*, and he sang the old ballad of Tam-lin, the story of Janet, a young woman who has a child with an otherworldly man in the forest. Songs, like folk tales are full of strange, enchanted, abusive men who appear from nowhere.

Well, the old couple loved Iain's stories, and John fetched his bottle of finest malt whisky and offered a very small dram. For three evenings, Iain told tales of his life at sea, of the kelpies and wulvers, and he showed them drawings of the weirdest fish. John asked what they tasted like, and Iain described it as a cross between a crookit mouth and a tammy harper. John wanted to know where to catch them, and Iain said the seals would lead them to the fishing grounds the following day. The old fisherman grumbled it was about time those seals made themselves useful, and he shook his fist at the pup in the cradle by the fire.

The following morning, the sky dawned clear, Mary packed a box with fresh oatcakes, plum jam and dulse, and told them to remember to offer a little to the sea. The two men sailed on the early morning tide, and soon their nets writhed with herring and mackerel and the pots rattled with lobsters and crabs.

Iain said they had caught enough, but John insisted on sailing further, for he wanted to taste these strange new fish. Iain looked up, there was a storm brewing, but the old man couldn't see the fish for the sea and he set sail. When the storm hit, a wave rocked the boat and Iain was tossed overboard.

John held out his hand, but the sea churned, and Iain had vanished. The old fisherman turned the boat for home, but another wave hit, and he too was drawn under the waves. He came up and gasped for air, once, twice, and he knew when he sank for the third time he would never see the sky again. He had thought of this moment and accepted his fate, but as he sank into the boiling waters, two arms wrapped around his waist.

When he awoke, he was lying on the shingle below his cottage. The storm had blown out, and Mary was pressing water from his lungs. He asked if Iain was safe, but Mary had not seen him. She lifted her man in her arms and carried him home, laid him down on Iain's bed, wiped the fever from his brow and fetched a doctor from the town.

John told Mary and the doctor what had happened and asked again if there was any sign of Iain. The doctor was curious to know who this mysterious young man was, so they told him how Iain was sent to them.

The doctor picked up a small canvas leaning against the wall behind the door. It was a painting of the seashore with the cottage in the background and an old woman collecting dulse in a leather apron, and in her arms was a seal pup. Mary watched the doctor's eyes to see if he understood. For she had always known that Iain was one of the unseen, a seal man, a silkie. The silkies always came when lessons were to be learned.

The doctor declared it a fine painting but explained that as far as he knew there had been no strangers in the town. He stared knowingly at Mary. She smiled, thanked him for his kindness and pushed him out the door, for she was sure he had many sick folk in need of his services.

As John slept calmly upstairs, Mary watched the seal pup in the cradle by the fire. It was grown enough to be returned to the sea. She wrapped it in her apron, walked down to the beach and left the pup where she had found it. The head of a seal bobbed up and down in the waves. It swam towards the shore, dragged itself onto the shingle and led its child back into the sea. They swam to the spot where the painting was made and vanished beneath the waves.

Old John, when he was back on his feet again, never knew he had been saved by a silkie, and Mary kept her silence. Neither did he know that fifty years before, she had come from the sea to marry him, when he was a kindhearted young fisherman who never took more herring than he needed and always offered a few back to the sea to thank his friends, the seals.

3

Boggart Hole Clough

ngland is an insular, divided land that has forgotten its myths,
separated now from the rest of Europe, clinging to an idealised
colonial past while celebrating the new gods of reality TV and
celebrity entrepreneurs. Its awkward relationship with its mythology
was symbolised back in 1917 by Sir Arthur Conan Doyle, creator
of the logician Sherlock Holmes, who wrote an article about fairies
illustrated with genuine photographs of gossamer-winged cardboard
cut-outs painted by two girls from Cottingley, Yorkshire, in a style
influenced by Doyle's father Charles and his uncle Richard, both
renowned Victorian fairy artists. Charles suffered from epilepsy,
amnesia, alcoholism and depression in his later years, and was sent
by his family to a 'home for intemperate gentlemen' and then to an
asylum where he continued to paint fairies and a set of illustrations
for his son's first novel, *A Study in Scarlet*.

I went to college in Manchester in the mid-1970s, when the
industrial north-west saw itself as a separate land to the posh south,
and the teaching of radical history and arts was flourishing. L.S.
Lowry was a secret known only within the city, the Royal Exchange
Theatre opened in a futuristic studio constructed inside the old
Corn Exchange, and Eddie and Ruth Frow founded the Working
Class Movement Library in their terraced house in Old Trafford.

I lived near Boggart Hole Clough, a municipally tamed urban park
with domesticated boggarts that was once a dark place shrouded in
mist. The clough was widely believed to be named after a mischievous
boggart who haunted George Cheetham's farm in Blackley, where
it snatched bread and butter from children's mouths, threw milk
around, made loud noises in the night and peeped through a hole in a
wooden partition, hence Boggart 'Hole' Clough.

This plausible legend was first published in 1829 by John Roby
in *Traditions of Lancashire*, although his source was Thomas Crofton
Croker, an Irish antiquarian who had once included a collection

of Welsh folk tales in his *Fairy Traditions of the South of Ireland*, without acknowledgement to Maria Jane Williams of Aberpergwm, who had gathered them around Glynneath in Wales. Roby's boggart legend bears an eerie resemblance to Maria Jane's Welsh tales, and anyway, the locals knew another story.

Boggart Hole Clough was a favourite childhood haunt of Samuel Bamford, weaver, poet, writer, historian and social reformer. On the morning of 16 August 1819, Samuel led 6,000 people down Rochdale Road, across Boggart Hole Clough to St Peter's Field in central Manchester, where 60,000 had gathered to listen to the orator Henry Hunt. They were there to protest about unemployment in the aftermath of the Napoleonic Wars, high food costs caused by the corn laws, and a lack of parliamentary representation. The peaceful meeting was attacked by armed cavalry, leaving hundreds injured and fifteen dead, forever remembered as the Peterloo Massacre.

Samuel was arrested, charged with riot and sentenced to a year in Lincoln Prison. On his release, he and his wife Jemima rented a cottage on the edge of Boggart Hole Clough, where he wrote a story that suggests the boggarts were not cartoonish elves, but mysterious people from another world.

South of Blackley, just off the road from Rochdale to Manchester, was a deep, forested gorge, entered by a white gate hung on whale-jaw posts. A desolate house stood there, built of old-fashioned bricks round a timber frame, so scary it was known as Fyrin-ho, or Boggart Hole, and the valley around was called Fyrin-ho' Kloof, or Boggart Hole Clough.

George Plant of Blackley was a sorcerer and a scientist, a firm believer in ghosts, witches and boggarts, a self-taught herbalist and self-confessed dreary-minded wanderer of lonely dells in search of plants to make into concoctions and potions. *Yarbin' eawt*, he called it, 'herbing out', and his favourite haunt was Fyrin-ho' Kloof, where he had discovered a patch of Saint John's Fern, or St John's Wort, which he believed cured all kinds of misery and melancholy. He knew the story of Roby's mischievous boggart, who he categorised as a species of German elf related to those recorded by the Brothers Grimm, although the Lancashire version probably referred to Ginny Greenteeth, who lived in stagnant ponds and took pleasure in drowning people.

One day, George was herbing in Gristlehurst Wood, near Birtle, when a storm broke. He knocked on the door of a cottage and asked a middle-aged woman for shelter. She invited him in, hung his coat to dry, threw coal and rootstocks on the fire, and sat him down with a bread flake filled with oat cakes, bacon, potatoes and a mug of beer. He realised this was a hush-shop, a house that doubled as an inn, so he ordered more ale and bacon and counted his money.

Sat by the window mending a pair of clogs was the woman's only son, Bangle, a morose red-haired lad of eighteen. He looked up as the door opened and another boy, short and dark, entered carrying two birdcages and a pot of lime. Clearly a bird-catcher.

'Eh up, Chirrup,' said Bangle. 'Caught owt?'

'I saw a right bonny bird. It weren't a gorse-cock, ouzel or dunnock, it were all golden yellow.'

'Show us?' asked Bangle

'Can't. It gorra way,' replied Chirrup.

'I suspect it was a yellow wagtail,' suggested George.

Bangle's mother explained, 'Look at 'em. One of 'em can't catch birds, and t'other's mopin' for a woman. Hopeless, the pair of 'em.'

'I may be able to help,' said George. 'I know herbalism and botany and make potions that cure ailments of the heart.'

'You some kind o' quack doctor?' asked Bangle's mum as she poured George a jug of beer and explained that her son was smitten with a girl who worked on a small cattle farm on Old Birtle Hill, but he was too shy to speak to her. And when he saw her dancing with another at Bury Fair, he came over melancholic.

Bangle's mother was fed up with him moping around, so she'd dragged him to see Limping Billy, the Radcliffe cunning man. Billy lived in a dimly lit room at the top of some steep steps, with a bed in one corner covered by old sacking, which was doubtless responsible for the musty smell. He sat at a wobbly table lit by a single candle, knees up to his chin, telling the fortunes of two entranced young women.

Bangle giggled. The conjurer glared and told him to sling his hook. Bangle's mother explained the problem, and Billy told them to make a potion from St John's Wort seed, which ought to put the smile on his face. Though, he added, it was best not to meddle with the Otherworld, or they might get a cob on. Then he charged them sixpence and explained to the two captivated girls how they would meet their sweethearts.

George told the boys about the patch of Saint John's Fern in Boggart Hole Clough, but he agreed with Billy that changing the natural ways with potions and spells can have strange side-effects, so they must each bring a counter-spell, something brown, something bright, and something deep. And they resolved to meet on St John's Eve.

So, a little before midnight on 23 June, the three men stood by the whale-jaw gate outside Fyrin-ho Kloof. George had brought an earthen dish that was brown enough; Chirrup, a pewter plate bright enough; and Bangle, a musty, tanned skull deep enough – it was sawn off above the eyes, the lid hinged with a piece of tanned scalp, and the cavity stuffed with moss and clay mixed with his own blood and three long raven hairs from his beloved given to him by an old woman who knew her.

They entered the gates and crossed the brook on the stepping stones below the spooky Fyrin house.

Bangle broke the silence. 'There's boggarts come out at night 'ere.'

Chirrup added, 'Aye. They pull children down holes.'

'An' a troll lives under the footbridge by the ninety-nine steps. We'll have to pay him or climb up and make a wish,' said Bangle

'A boggart had a fight with a big chap from Blackley. There's bits of its body here, look, a tooth and a foot,' added Chirrup, pointing at some stones.

'An' there's Ginny Greenteeth …'

'Hush,' said George, 'There are greater forces at work than Ginny Greenteeth. There are fairies here, brought by Morgana le Fey.'

'Fairies?' giggled Chirrup.

'Who's Morgana when she's at 'ome?' sniggered Bangle.

They crossed the White Moss, through the plantation and followed the stream past the tracks to Booth Hall and The Bell in Moston, until they came to a clearing circled by ancient oaks, hazel and ash, tangled with bramble, rose, holly and clumps of unusual ferns, pale green and standing rigid, like something had terrified them – Saint John's Ferns.

An eerie silence clung in the air. Not even the hoot of an owl, the moan of the wind or the howl of a banshee.

George told them not to touch. He cut a cleft stick of witch hazel, held his dish under the plant and shook the stem.

Chirrup held his plate below, and Bangle placed the skull beneath.

As the fern seed fell into the dish, George incanted, 'Good St John, this seed we crave. We have come, so leave your grave.'

Darkness clawed at them. A breeze blew from nowhere. The dish exploded, the pewter plate melted, and the skull's eyes glared in its sockets.

'I'm feart!' said Bangle.

'Scarper!' said Chirrup.

'Look!' said George.

They were surrounded by women and children dressed in old clothes, walking, drifting, singing mournfully, shrouded in a dream of an idealised past.

The wind ripped the air and the trees moaned as if they were being wrenched from the earth.

The boggarts emerged from the bushes, their shapes indiscernible, watching, smiling, threatening. The three men couldn't tell if they were friendly, but they were from t'Otherworld and this was their worst nightmare.

They ran in three different directions.

George headed towards the old house, leapt over the brook, looked over his shoulder to find he was being chased by something part human, gnashing its teeth and howling. He woke at home in a fever, not knowing how he got there.

Chirrup was found on the White Moss, chasing birds and gibbering madly about yellow wagtails. He spent the remainder of his manic life in Crumpsall Hospital painting fairies.

Bangle ran home clutching the skull, as its eyes burned into his soul. He buried it at the crossroads with some seeds, and later that evening his lover appeared by his bedside. The boggarts had granted his wish.

And a few days later, Bangle's new lover walked behind his coffin as he was laid in the gravel.

4

The Glashtyn

In the 1940s, as a bus crossed the Fairy Bridge over Santon Burn in Ellan Vannin, the Isle of Man, the driver with tongue in cheek asked the passengers to say, '*Laa Mie*' ('Hello Fairies'). These days, a pre-recorded voice says, 'Please serve the Manx tradition, and say "Hi Fairies" as we cross the Fairy Bridge' – otherwise, you might catch chicken pox or be responsible for a crash during the TT Races.

The bridge is hung with teddy bears, love messages and underwear, leather-clad bikers take selfies by the fairy road sign, while local schoolchildren decorate the Real Fairy Bridge further along the burn. They are known as *mooinjer veggey* in Manx, or the 'li'l fallas', the crowd, the mob, and they still peep through the fog of wealth from their hiding place behind the offshore tax avoidance schemes, insurance companies, online gamblers and IT firms.

In 1911, Sophia Morrison published a book of *Manx Fairy Tales* containing stories of *mooinjer veggey*, along with the mermaid of Gob ny Ooyl and the Buggane of Glen Meay Waterfall. Ms Morrison lived in a row of houses built by her father, a fisherman in Peel. She was a musician, writer and editor of the cultural magazine *Mannin* and founder of the Manx Language Society, *Yn Çheshaght Ghailckagh*. The last native speaker passed away in 1974, leaving the language officially extinct, to the surprise of the schoolchildren at Bunscoill Ghaelgagh, who wrote to UNESCO explaining that they could write and speak Manx along with 2,000 others. One is a friend from Yorkshire who lives in Brittany and also speaks Breton, Irish and Welsh.

Stories weave the Celtic languages together. I knew the tale of the Water Horse, *Ceffyl Dŵr*, from Wales, and then heard Cat Weatherill's contemporary Manx version, which has influenced my retelling, along with a brief reference in the folklore of the Isle of Man, written in 1891 by the politician A.W. Moore, and Sofia

Morrison's 'great, big ugly beast of a Buggane', who carries a lazy woman called Kirry away to the Glen Meay Waterfall. It explains why living on an island surrounded by sea can be so scary. The answer is not to be afraid.

Once upon a full moon, a widow woman lived in a cottage at the end of the lane that leads down to the pebble beach near Glion Meay. She took in washing, cleaned floors, darned socks – any job that earned a few pennies to keep her family. See her daughters in the bed? Count them: *nane, jees, tree, kiare*.

Her eldest was Cara, the songbird, a practical girl who chopped wood with one swing of the axe, stared out polecats when they came sniffing round the chickens, and had a cat with a stump for a tail. While mother was at work, Cara looked after her sisters. She fetched spring water from the well on the hill, warmed it in a pan over the fire and bathed them till they shone. She cooked soup with special herbs she grew on the croft, and then she hurried them upstairs, tucked them into bed and sang songs about the Buggane to terrify them to sleep.

It was Twelfth Night, old Christmas, when mischief and misrule were in the air, and creatures passed from one world to the other, when mother said to Cara, 'I've a new job, with a gentleman in Douglas, a kind man who pays well, and he's asked me to work tonight, so I must stay till morning. You understand? Look after your sisters while I'm gone, don't scare 'em with your tales of the *Fynoderee* or *Mooinjer Veggey*, and don't open the door to any handsome strangers that look like stallions. They might be the Howler, the Buggane, the Cabbyl-Ushtey, or worse, the Glashtyn. Remember that poor soul who drowned at the waterfall? They collected up the pieces in a bucket!'

Mother parted her daughter's black hair in the middle and wove it into plaits, and that frosty afternoon she set off, rouge on her lips, blusher on her cheeks and hair tied in a bunch. Cara thought mother had never looked so beautiful. She bathed her sisters, made soup with the special herbs and told them about a Glashtyn who carried children away on its back until a brave girl came along and chopped it into pieces and boiled it up for glue. Then she tucked them into bed, kissed them goodnight and left them to their night-mares. She settled down in the stick chair by the hearth with a mug of hot chocolate and her book of Manx folk tales, lit the candle and read about the mermaid of Gob-ny-Ooyl.

Cara had drifted off to sleep when she was awoken by a rat-a-tat-tat on the door. She put down her mug, pinned her plaits into a bunch and clutched her book to her chest so the stories would protect her from whatever was lurking outside. She picked up the poker, went to the door and whispered, 'Who's knocking so late?'

There was a sound of snorting, a rustling of hooves and a voice, 'Only a weary traveller who means the lady of the house no harm.'

The cat hissed and bristled and would have thrashed its tail if only it had one.

Gripping the poker tightly behind her back, Cara lifted the latch, and oh, her heart missed a beat. There stood the most delicious young man, with deep eyes, high cheekbones and a smile of shining white teeth that made her legs melt. Though they were particularly big teeth.

'Bon soir, mademoiselle,' he smiled lopsidedly as he brushed his long hair from his eyes. 'I have returned from the sea, and was passing by your house when I saw a flickering candle and thought to myself, I am sure the handsome young lady who lives there will give me food for my groaning belly and perhaps a place to rest my head by her fireside?'

Cara, raised on fairy tales and woodcutting as she was, knew this was the Glashtyn, come to carry her sisters away on his back and drop them into the depths of the ocean. But he was pretty in that floppy-haired English way, and despite the warning voice in her head, she found herself saying, 'Come in'.

The Glashtyn rushed past her, settled himself by the open hearth, took a swig of Cara's chocolate and wiped his mouth on a sleeve. She hid the poker behind the door in case she needed to crack his head open like an eggshell.

She offered him the remains of the soup she had made for her sisters, which he gulped down greedily, rubbed his belly, slobbered and snorted. In between mouthfuls, he told her he was a sailor who had been to places Cara could only dream of, with names she could never pronounce, and all the while she longed to stroke that long silky hair he swept from his eyes.

Cara was a practical girl. You remember the herbs she had cooked in the soup? The special herbs from the croft? Well, they were the secret ingredient designed to send her sisters to sleep. Cara had no wish to stay up all night reading them stories when there was hot chocolate to drink, books to read and dreams to dream. And, sure as snow is frozen tears, the Glashtyn was dozing in the stick chair, head flopping backwards and forwards in time with his snoring.

Cara so wanted to plait his mane and bind it into a ponytail. One stroke wouldn't do any harm, would it? She stood up, took a step forward, and stretched out her hand, but there was nothing silky in this mane, it was rough and gritty, no, not grit, coarse sand and broken seashells. She felt something hairy, long and pointy, a horse's ear. She let go as if it was hag-ridden, took a step back and sat down.

The cat jumped on her lap and dug in its claws. Make no noise, mustn't wake him. He's a Glashtyn, he will eat her up or lift her skirt or carry her to his underwater stable and she will grow gills and fins and be covered in seaweed and limpets, and never see her family again.

In the pause between heartbeats, she heard the lapping of the waves on the shell of a long-dead crab and the breathing of a silverfish behind the bookcase. The cat so wanted to flick the Glashtyn's ear with its paw. Every second lasted a minute, every minute an hour.

And then … CRACK … a blazing log leapt from the fire. His eyes opened and his charming smile became that of a predator's, with shiny white teeth that bite. He stood up, his neck arched over, his sandy mane blew in the hot air from the fire, he opened his mouth wider, and she could smell his horsey breath as he stood over her like a giant chess piece about to take a pawn.

Cara slowed her beating heart, reached out her arm, stroked his mane, rubbed his long nose, kissed his mouth full of teeth, sat in the stick chair by the fire, opened her book, placed an apple in his hoof and told him the story of the Mermaid of Gob-ny-Ooyl.

The Glashtyn curled up at her feet, and bit into the apple.

'Once, a mermaid haunted Bulgham Bay and brought luck to the Sayle family who lived at Cornaa. One spring day, Evan, the eldest boy, a clever lad, saw the mermaid sitting on the rock. He left an apple on the beach for her.

'She ate the apple, and sang:

> The luck o' the sea be with you, but don't forgetful be
> Of bringing some sweet land-eggs for the children of the sea.

'Next day, Evan filled his boat with apples and the mermaid swam to him and gathered them in her arms:

> The luck o' the sea be with you, but don't forgetful be
> Of bringing some sweet land-eggs for the children of the sea.

'Come the autumn, Evan decided to leave Vannin forever. Before he left, he planted an apple tree at Bulgham so the mermaid would always have land-eggs. Each year she sang:

> The luck o' the sea be with you, but don't forgetful be
> Of bringing some sweet land-eggs for the children of the sea.

'And the old tree is still there at Gob-ny-Ooyl, the Point of Apples.'

There was a crack of thunder. Cara looked out of the window as day broke. She took hold of the poker, flung the door wide and the morning sun slithered across the step like a slug. The Glashtyn grabbed the hem of Cara's skirt. The cat jumped on his back and sunk in her claws.

A shaft of light caught him on the side of his neck. He threw his head back and howled. Cara tore her skirt free of his grip, and with his arms flailing by his side, he galloped his long legs through the door, and the last Cara heard was the sound of hooves on pebbles and a voice singing, '*Rumbyl, rumbyl, sambyl*'.

She ran to the shoreline and peered into the dark water, but all she saw were the white horses, the waves, lapping up on the shore, kissing her bare feet. Cara would have strange tales to tell in the morning.

But then, so would her mother.

5

The Sceach and the Seanchaí

A few years ago, I was working at the Ennis Street Arts Festival in County Clare and was staying just over the border in the old barrack town of Ardrahan, near Coole in County Galway, where I was house-sitting a friend's flock of chickens and handmade puppets.

One hundred years earlier, Lady Augusta Gregory turned her home at Coole Park into a meeting place for the Irish Literary Revival as part of the movement towards political and cultural independence. She wrote about the folk culture of Clare and Galway, from Biddy Early, the healing woman of Kinvara, to the *droch fhola*, the dead who returned vampirically for blood, and the *raths*, fairy forts, iron-age mounds as important as any stately castle or great painting. It's not considered wise to damage a fairy fort, as the wealthy entrepreneur Seán Quinn discovered when he went bankrupt after moving one near his home in Cavan.

While exploring the *raths* around Ardrahan, being careful not to disturb the hidden people, I heard a story about a hawthorn tree that stood on the County Clare side of the border near Lough Bunny in the Burren. The council decided to take it down to make way for a road, but the poorly paid lads in the road gang stood around holding their cross-cuts, talking and shaking their heads. The foreman asked what they were doing, and they said they weren't going to touch a lone *sceach gheal*. There would be trouble. The *sióga* would be angry.

The foreman, a practical man, said there was nothing supernatural about the tree, or the surveyor would have noticed. One of the lads said the surveyor worked at a desk in an office in Ennis and wouldn't know about things like this. Another said he'd read about a lone *sceach* in one of Lady Gregory's books, and a third said it would be best not to mess with Them.

The foreman explained that if they didn't cut down the thorn tree, they'd be out of work come the evening, and he'd have no trouble

replacing them, for jobs were scarce now the meat factory had closed in Gort, and the unemployed Brazilians who had worked there could easily be retrained to handle a cross-cut. Still, the men shuffled and muttered, and the foreman realised his own job was on the line. So, he picked out two lads with young families who couldn't afford to lose wages and ordered them to pick up the cross-cut.

They reluctantly sawed into the trunk, but after two draws, their jaws dropped to the ground, and they stepped back. The tree was bleeding. They saw it with their own eyes. There was no sound, just blood pouring from the cut. And none of those lads would touch it after that, not even the foreman.

This sort of thing has happened all over Ireland, for while few would admit they believe in the fairies, no one with any sense would cut down a lone *sceach gheal*. Thomas Moorhead of Killanena cut one with an axe and came down with a headache and a nosebleed and took to his bed for three weeks. John Judge cut another in Coolnaha, and all his hair fell out. At Ferenka in Limerick they replanted one, but the town had nothing but bad luck from that day. And even those on the northern side of the border that separates the Republic from the British weren't immune.

In the mid-1970s, the Detroit engineer and entrepreneur John DeLorean opened a car plant in Dunmurry to manufacture his two-seater gull-winged sports car. A lone hawthorn stood in the field where the plant was to be built, and the construction workers refused to take it down. DeLorean knew nothing of the stories of the *sceach*, so he climbed into a bulldozer and flattened the tree himself. By 1982, half of his 7,000 cars remained unsold, the company was $175 million in debt, the Dunmurry factory was in receivership, and DeLorean was arrested and charged for tax evasion, defrauding investors and smuggling cocaine. He was eventually cleared, but only after the little people had their fun.

The magical old ways of the *Gaeltacht* and the Irish Gaelic, *Gaelige nah Éireann*, are close to the surface here. For without magic, it would be a terribly sad place, so says the *seanchaí*, storyteller, teacher and writer, Eddie Lenihan, who has spent much of his life telling tales of the little people to a world increasingly out of touch with the old ways and the land.

He has recorded stories from the old people throughout his life, so many that he thinks it would take another lifetime to catalogue, transcribe and archive them. So, he has gathered some together in books, including the classic *Meeting the Other Crowd*, in which Carolyn Ann Green writes that meeting him for the first time was not unlike encountering one of Them. So perhaps it's not surprising that over the years, tales have begun to be told about Mr Lenihan himself, for he reminds the Irish people of what they are in danger of losing. He told me this tale himself over lunch in a café in Crusheen while I was working in Ennis.

One day in 1999, Eddie was driving through Latoon on his way home from Limerick where he was teaching at the High School, when he noticed some men in a field called Lynch's Crag where a lone *sceach* stood. He stopped the car and asked what they thought they were doing, and they explained they were constructing the new 20-million-euro EU-funded Ennis bypass.

Eddie asked if they were concerned about their excavations. They looked at one another blankly as he explained that this thorn tree was where the fairies of Munster laid out their war dead after the battles with the fairies of Leinster. It was a burial site. Lumps of green were found there. Fairy blood. It would not be wise to let anything happen to that tree, or innocent motorists could be in danger when the other crowd took revenge. And he had seen a black dog along this route. He warned them, 'I wouldn't want to be in your shoes!'

In the face of the little people, the workmen laid down their tools, while Eddie wrote a letter to the local newspaper and was interviewed on radio and in the *Irish Times*, which led to people writing and phoning in support of the *seanchaí*. A quarter-page article in the *New York Times* followed and soon over forty newspapers in the USA and Europe ran the story, along with twelve TV stations across the USA, Canada and Europe. Mr Lenihan was standing in the way of unnecessary modernity and was not alone.

No one dared touch the *sceach*. The National Road Authority reached a compromise. The bypass was built, but to a new route that bypassed the proposed bypass around the fairy-thorn of Latoon, although this wasn't the end of the matter. In August 2002, under cover of darkness, a man took a chainsaw to the tree, leaving only the trunk standing. The press phoned Eddie and asked if the perpetrator was still alive. He replied that he had no way of knowing, for only those around him knew if there had been recrimination. If he was to be saved, he would need something holy, dirty, red, salty, as well as fire, water and some other stuff.

The evening after I met Eddie in Crusheen, I found myself in a music session back in Ardrahan. The man sat next to me told me he was an archaeologist who carried out site surveys before roads and houses were built, and he had worked on the Ennis bypass. So, I asked him about the Latoon *sceach*.

He smiled, 'Ah, Mr Lenihan is well respected round here, everyone listens to his words. He knows far more than a mere archaeologist.'

A big rugby-playing teenager sat next to us agreed and said that he had been sceptical, but his sister convinced him to believe in the fairies. So, I asked the archaeologist what he had found during the dig, and he explained they had carbon-dated the tree, so I asked, 'How old is the *sceach*?'

He grinned, 'About fifty years. The 1960s.'

You see, people only hear what they want to hear. Mr Lenihan told everyone, quite clearly and correctly, that a man, just one man, had told him the tale of the fairy-tree of Latoon. And that was enough.

However, Eddie knew the story spoke a deeper, emotional truth beyond the literal one, about the damage caused to the environment without a thought to the past. There is a need to believe in the quiet people, and the *seanchaí* gives them a voice, memories of the old ways that allow changes for the better, rather than for the sake of it.

By way of an afterword

Twenty-eight years after it was first proposed, the controversial M4 relief road south of Newport in South Wales was cancelled due to escalating costs by the new First Minister, Mark Drakeford, from Carmarthenshire, a stronghold of the Tylwyth teg.

6

The Stonewaller and the Korrigan

BREIZH, BRITTANY

Sioni Winwns, or Johnny Onions in English, used to call at my mam's house on Pen Llŷn with strings of Breton onions draped across the handlebars of his bicycle. Mam invited him in, placed a *paned* of tea and an out-of-date cake from the *Gwalia* on the kitchen table for him, while he hung a string of onions in the cupboard under the stairs for her. He spoke a little Welsh and English, and was well loved in the village, but he wasn't the only *Sioni*.

Onion sellers first travelled from Brittany around 200 years ago, and by 1900 over 1,000 spent their winters cycling round Wales and formed themselves into companies with their own sales territory. The man who visited my mam came from a business in Porthmadog run by Welsh-speaking Claude Deridan from Roscoff.

A few years ago, another, less stereotypical, itinerant Breton man appeared in Wales. Samuel Allo, troubadour, storyteller and singer, is rooted in the old oral tradition of travelling educator. He has told stories to schoolchildren all over the world, and wherever he stays, he makes a meal, sings a song and tells a tale in exchange for a place to lay his head. His storytelling is from the same landscape as the Finistère author Emile Souvestre, who wrote *Le Foyer Breton* in 1844, and Anatole Le Braz, bard of Brittany and Professor of French Literature at the University of Rennes, who collected tales of the dead in *La légende de la mort en Basse-Bretagne* in 1902, which was translated into English by the folk tale scholar, publisher, writer and my neighbour from across the valley, Derek Bryce.

On Samuel's first visit to West Wales, he told a story heard from the old man who taught him to speak Breton. Samuel also tells tales of the Korrigan, the ankou, and other characters from the Breton Otherworld, and all of them have crept into this retelling.

A young couple lived in a ramshackle stone cottage at the foot of a hill in Morbihan with their baby boy, but as the child grew, they realised something was wrong. He wasn't a changeling child, or a wild boy like Yannick, or a child who cried like a cat. He simply never spoke. His parents encouraged him, showed him objects, used sign language, but by the time he was three, no words had passed his lips.

One day, they sat him by the front door and gave him some pebbles to play with. He stared at the hills for an age, then picked up a stone, warmed it in his chubby hands, turned it over and placed it upon another. Day after day, he piled stone upon stone, carefully ensuring each shape interlocked with the next. It came as no surprise to the villagers that the child grew into a strong and silent young man who earned his living as a drystone-waller.

He built the straightest walls in Brittany, as if he had drawn a line with a ruler over hilltops and through woods, without a curve or bend, and he never used a plumbline or spirit level. The villagers admired his skill, but they knew walls could only be straight with the agreement of the Korrigan, the unseen people. If the Korrigan refused access across their land, the wall must be built around them. That's why walls have wobbles.

One evening as autumn melted into winter, shouting was heard from the hillside, followed by the rumbling of rock, a crash that echoed through the air, then a deafening silence. The villagers knew the wall builder had argued with the stones who had refused to cross the Korrigans' land, and the wall had collapsed, crushing him.

The Korrigan gathered round his broken body. The Kornikaneds of the forests joined them, along with the Korils from the heaths and groves, the Poulpikans of the marshes, and the Teuz, the black elves of the meadows and wheatfields. They had told him many times not to cross their land while they hibernated through the winter. And now he had built his wall across the clearing where they danced. He had been warned.

The Korrigan were clearing the stones from his body when they heard a voice.

'Leave him. Go to sleep in your burrows. That boy is mine.'

A small woman stood there, dressed in white, carrying a laundry basket on her head, and her feet were webbed.

'It's the night duck,' shouted one Korrigan.

'She'll break our arms,' said another.

'She'll prophecy our deaths,' trembled a third.

And they vanished in the blink of an eye.

This was Kannerezed Noz, one of *la lavandiéres de nuits*, the night washerwomen. She looked at the stonewaller, placed her wrist by his mouth to search for breath, and threw the rest of the stones from his body as if they were pebbles.

'You've made a mess of yourself, my boy. We'll go to my house and wash the blood from your clothes, or they'll become your shroud,' and she sang as she removed his jacket and shirt:

Quen na zui kristen salver
Rede goëlc'hi hou licer
Didan an earc'h ag an aër.

[Until a Christian saves us, we must scrub your shroud white as the snow and the wind.]

She was tugging his trousers down when she heard the rattling of a horse and cart.

'Leave him. Go to your wash house, old woman. He is mine.'

The washerwoman turned to see an old black horse harnessed to a rickety black cart driven by a tall black-cloaked figure with a wide-brimmed hat pulled down to hide her eyes.

'*War ma fé, heman zo eun Ankou drouk!*' said the washerwoman. ('On my faith, it's a nasty Ankou!')

Ankou, the watcher of graveyards, who accompanied lost souls to the land of the dead. The washerwoman knew there were few souls more lost than hers, so she vanished, still clutching the young man's trousers.

Ankou towered over the stonewaller, kicked him to check for life, and pulled down her hood to reveal a white skull that revolved, slowly and disturbingly.

'You aren't dead enough. Breathe out, leave your body, and I will take you to my friend, Death. Hurry, I finish work in half an hour, and I have a ticket for the Seventh Seal.'

The stonewaller coughed, sat up and stared at Ankou with a look that said, 'I am not ready to meet Death.'

'Yes, you are. Sign here!' and she produced a contract from her cloak, gave the stonewaller a pen, and pointed to where it said, 'on behalf of the customer'.

The stonewaller shook his head.

'A digital signature will do,' said Ankou, holding out her smartphone.

Then she picked him up and whirled him round in a dance of death.

There was a crash, Ankou stopped dancing, and turned to see the axle of her cart had been broken and the wheel was hanging off. A young woman, wearing a headscarf and baggy trousers, was standing by the cart holding a staff.

'Leave him. Go back to the Dead. The boy is mine!'

'You've broken my cart. Maybe I'll take you instead,' said Ankou.

The woman took a rope from her shoulder, and holding the cart up with one hand, tied the wheel back onto the axle.

Ankou knew this was a Mazzer, a dream-hunter, probably not local, from Corsica or the submerged land of Kêr-Is. Ankou pulled her hood over her skull to avoid the dream-hunter's eyes, climbed onto the cart, grabbed the reins and was gone.

The dream-hunter turned the stonewaller's face to hers and stared into his eyes.

'I don't know you. You'll live, but someone must die in your place,' and she sprang to her feet and disappeared into the forest.

The dream-hunter had not chosen to be a Mazzer. She lived in a hut on the marginal world between the living and the dead. She kept a few sheep and goats and hunted wild boar. People avoided her gaze, for they knew she had the power of life and death.

She heard the villagers climbing the hill in search of the stone-waller. She watched as they gently laid him on a wooden bier and carried him home. She saw one man was diseased and would be dead within days. His life in exchange for the stonewaller's.

The villagers didn't see the Mazzer because she wasn't there. She was at home in bed, dreaming. When she awoke, she milked her goats, gathered a few eggs for breakfast, settled down by the fire with a coffee and read her book of love stories.

Although the young man's body was badly broken, his parents cared for him until his bones slowly mended. They sat him by the front door to feel the sun on his face. He stared at the hill, then raised his arm, and despite the pain, picked up a stone, smelled it, stroked it in his enormous palm and placed it upon another.

Soon he was stonewalling once more, but he never built a straight wall again, and the villagers knew by the bends and kinks and wobbles, that he finally understood that the stones would never cross the unseen land of the Korrigan.

7

Schneeweißchen
und Rosenroot

Dortchen Wild was born in Kassel in 1893 and grew up telling fairy tales to her five sisters as they sat spinning and sewing round the hearth, while French troops occupied her town and Napoleon's brother, Jérôme Bonaparte, was crowned King of Westphalia. When her sisters left home, she was left alone with an abusive father who disliked his daughter fraternising with the poor folk next door.

Little wonder she preferred the company of Rumpelstiltskin, the Frog King, the Elves and the Shoemaker, Sweetheart Roland, Mother Holle, the Singing Bones, All-Kinds-of-Fur, the Singing Springing Lark and Hansel and Gretel. She told these tales to her next-door neighbour and closest friend, Lotte Grimm, who had been left orphaned in Steinau before moving to Kassel with her brothers Wilhelm and Jacob.

The two young Grimm Brothers wrote down Dortchen's stories, fearing they would be lost forever during the occupation by the French Army, and they published them in their international best-seller, *Kinder und Hausmärchen* in 1812. Thirteen years later, with both her father and Bonaparte gone, Dortchen married Wilhelm and moved in with the Grimm siblings, but she remained in their shadows, even though a quarter of the tales in her husband's book came from her lips. Her name was as hidden as Rumpelstiltskin's, at least until Kate Forsyth published her biographical novel, *The Wild Girl*.

'*Die Wichtelmänner*', 'The Elves and the Shoemaker', became the universal blueprint for the helpful, mischievous little people (I illustrated this for Ladybird Books back in the 1990s, but that's a whole other story). Amidst criticism that their otherworldly characters were too dark and scary, the Grimms included more child-friendly stories in their seventh edition in 1857. One of these was '*Der undankbare Zwerg*' ('The Ungrateful Dwarf'), which Wilhelm read in a book of fables published in 1816 by Karoline Stahl, yet another mysterious hidden woman. He renamed it '*Schneeweißchen und Rosenrot*', 'Snow White and Rose Red', the tale of a child-unfriendly-elf-neighbour-from-hell.

A white rose tree and a red rose tree stood either side of the door of a cottage where a mother lived with her two daughters on the edge of the forest. Snow White was a winter child, quiet and gentle, who curled up by the fire, watched the falling snow though the shutters and filled her sketchbook with drawings from the darker imaginings of her favourite fairytales. Rose Red was of the summer, wild and strong, who climbed trees, left bowls of freshly picked flowers on the kitchen table and licked drops of blood from her fingers when she pricked herself on pins.

They were so different they were exactly alike.

'We'll never be parted,' said Snow White.

'Not even by death,' said Rose Red, and they wove berries and ferns into their hair and slept in the forest in each other's arms, while the night creatures watched over them. They had no fear, these rose-sisters, for they were the forest itself, and had the protection of thorns.

One winter evening there was a knock on the door.

Rose Red lifted the latch, and a bear said, 'Please may I warm myself by your fire? I have icicles dripping from my nose.'

'Poor Bear,' said mother, 'lie in the cinders, and try not to set fire to your fur.'

Bear flopped down like a great hearth rug while Snow White and Rose Red crawled over him, beat the snow from his fur, brushed him till he was dry, rolled him around like a ball and warmed their feet on him. They sat by their spinning wheels and span the yarn of '*Die Wichtelmänner*' from their book of *Kinder und Hausmärchen*, the famous tale of two kind elves who help a poor shoemaker and his wife earn a living by sewing the most beautiful shoes.

A fug of steam rose from Bear's damp fur, 'I like that story, but the elves who live in my forest are not as kind as those who helped your shoemaker. They think they own all this land, and they are very rude.'

So, the rose-girls told him another story about a woman who span wool and he snorted with laughter when he heard the elf's name was Rumpelstiltskin.

Bear stayed all winter until he'd heard every story in the book, and when spring came, he said, 'I must go now. In winter the elves sleep underground, but now the snow is melting, they will crawl out and trash my forest unless I stop them. But I will return in autumn to hear your stories all over again.'

He rubbed noses with both girls and trundled off into the trees.

The rose-girls missed their friend, until one day they were collecting wood for the stove when they heard screaming and swearing. An elf was jumping up and down on a felled tree, shrieking because its long white beard was trapped beneath the trunk.

The elf glared at the girls through red eyes, 'Why are you standing there like two fence posts, you ugly creatures? Help my poor beard!'

'What were you doing, little man?' asked Rose Red.

'I'm not little, you bags of skin and bone!' shouted the elf. 'I'm a giant. I was cutting up this fallen tree to build a beautiful fence around my land to keep the bears out when it grabbed my beard. So rude! Did I tell you how ugly you are?'

'You did,' replied Snow White, and she grabbed the elf round the body, Rose Red took his ankles, the girls nodded and tugged, but he was wedged tight. So Snow White took her scissors and cut off the end of the elf's beard.

The elf turned orange in the face, 'My beard! My beautiful beard! So sad!'

'Don't be so ungrateful,' said Snow White.

'We set you free,' added Rose Red.

'No way! I freed myself! You snowflakes are as much use as the boil on my bottom! Now get off my land before I sue!' and the elf pulled a bag of gold from his pocket, stuck out his tongue and disappeared into the forest.

Well, the girls laughed, for this elf was the most selfish creature they had ever met. But then, they hadn't travelled much beyond the forest.

The following day, the rose-girls were fishing by the stream when the elf came running along the bank with its beard trailing in the water. They grabbed hold of it just before it fell in.

'Let me go, snowflakes!'

'You're going to drown,' said Snow White.

'You're so little,' said Rose Red.

'I'm not little! I'm a giant!' screamed the elf, 'I caught that fish with my beautiful beard and it's trying to drag me in the river! Rude fish!'

Rose Red took the scissors, cut off the rest of the elf's beard, and the pike swam away.

'My beautiful beard!' shrieked the elf, 'I might as well be dead without my beard!'

'That could be arranged,' said Rose Red, stroking the scissors.

'That pike was going to eat you. We saved you again,' said Snow White.

'No way! I was about to make that shark into saucrkraut! Now get off my river before I sue!' and the elf took its bag of gold, gave a rude sign, and vanished down a hole.

The girls laughed all the way home.

The following morning the rose-sisters were on their way to town when they saw a kestrel hover then drop to the ground and snatch up the elf in its talons. They shrugged their shoulders, grabbed the elf's legs and held on till the bird flew away.

The elf screamed, 'Oh, not you two smelly rose petals. You've torn my coat! Buy me a new one!'

'You ungrateful creep,' said Rose Red.

'You were about to be eaten,' added Snow White.

'No way! I was going to have that turkey for dinner! Now get out of my forest before I sue!' and the elf took his gold, thumbed his nose at the girls, and hid behind a rock.

The girls giggled all the way to town.

On the way home they heard more screaming and swearing, and there was their friend Bear holding the elf in his great paws.

The elf shouted, 'Don't stand there gawping, snowflowers. Free me from this fleabag.'

'We've saved you three times already,' said Snow White.

'You've used up all your lives, cat-boy,' said Rose Red.

The elf told Bear, 'I'm only little. Eat those two plump girls instead! And get off my land!'

Bear looked at the girls, who shrugged their shoulders, so he swallowed the elf whole, rubbed his belly, and belched. A muffled voice muttered something about making Elfland great again.

Silence filled the forest, at least until Bear's belly rumbled, his skin burst open and just as the girls expected his guts to fall out, an impossibly handsome man appeared.

'Who are you?' asked Snow White.

'What have you done to Bear?' said Rose Red.

He spoke, 'I'm a prince. I was walking through my forest looking for birds to shoot when that rude elf told me to get off his land. I informed him it was my land and drew my sword to chop off his head, when he turned me into a bear and stole my gold. And I'm free, thanks to you two snowflakes. Now get off my land!'

'Who says you own the forest?' asked Snow White.

'It belonged to my father, and my grandfather before him, and all my great grandfathers before them.'

'And how did they come to own it?' asked Rose Red.

'They fought for it, and won great battles.'

'Then we'll fight you for it!' and the rose-girls rolled up their sleeves, grabbed the man's arms, shoved him back into the bearskin and zipped it up. Bear sat up and they climbed all over his fur because they loved him more than any boring fairytale prince.

Bear gave Snow White and Rose Red the prince's gold, and they bought seeds for their mother's garden that grew into red and white and pink roses, and they made Bear a red jacket to keep him warm in winter while they tell him tales from their sister, Dortchen Wild.

And Bear was happier than he ever was as a prince, knowing that he didn't own the land. If anything, the land owned him.

8

A Tale of Tales

ITALIA, ITALY

Every winter my mother took me to the Italianate fairy-tale village of Portmeirion, a twentieth-century architectural fantasy on the north-west coast of Wales that took Clough Williams-Ellis over fifty years to design and build. It has attracted visitors the world over, including Noël Coward, Doctor Who and half the Beatles, though we were lured more by the free out-of-season entry for locals and especially the legendary Italian ice creams.

Welsh Italian ice cream originated with migrants like Artillo Conti, who came from Bardi to work as a woodsman in the 1930s but instead opened a café in Ystradgynlais, while Joe Cascarini followed his father Luigi from the Abruzzi Mountains to sell Joe's ice cream in St Helen's Road, Swansea. The Arcari family arrived in the early 1900s from the southern mountaintop village of Picinisco to their shop opposite the Swansea Palace Theatre.

The Piciniscani were poor farmers who had little prospect of owning their own businesses in a country run by feudal estates, so migration offered opportunities. For centuries, the picturesque images of drystone terraces and colourful villas inhabited by rustic fieldworkers, woodcutters and shepherds hid the secret world of the *mezzadri*, unpaid sharecroppers entrapped by wealthy aristocracy in a form of slavery that survived into the 1980s.

The story reached a wider audience in 2018 through Alice Rohrwacher's film *Lazzaro Felice* (*Happy as Lazzaro*), which told of the sharecroppers from the idyllic village of Inviolta who found further incarceration in the city, where they survived by eating wildflowers that grew in the urban dereliction.

Between 1634 and 1636, Giambattista Basile, poet, courtier, soldier and fairy tale collector from Naples, published *Lo cunto de li cunti overo lo trattenemiento de peccerille* (*The Tale of Tales*). One of his Neapolitan fairy stories was *La Schiavottella* [*The Slave Girl*], a story of *le persone nascoste*, the hidden people.

In the day of days, a seamstress was employed to lift her skirt at night for the Marquis of Serva-Scura, a morose man who knew little pleasure in his life. One evening, he challenged her to jump over a bouquet of roses on his bed without damaging the flowers. She ran the length of the room and cleared the bed, but as she landed, a solitary leaf fluttered silently to the ground. She swallowed it before the Marquis noticed.

After three months, a child grew in her belly. She asked advice of the fairy-girls who lived amongst the roses, and they told her this was no immaculate birth, for she was carrying a leaf-child, and its father was the Marquis.

After nine months she delivered a rose-girl, born with fragrance and thorns, and the fairy-girls named her Lisa. They hurried to bring her gifts and charms, but one slipped, twisted her foot, and accidentally cursed the child.

At the end of seven years, the curse came true. While the seamstress was combing her daughter's hair, the comb stuck fast, Lisa fell to the ground, and nothing would wake her. The fairy-girls laid her in a glass coffin and placed it within six more, one inside the other, and locked them in an attic room in the Marquis's house.

The seamstress, inconsolable at losing her only child, faded away, and so this tale of tales brought another death. The Marquis was plunged into greater misery, caused less by the loss of his mistress than worrying whether he could keep the estate running at a profit when those lazy sharecroppers who worked for him were robbing him of wine, tobacco and coffee. To ease his melancholy, he married the daughter of a rich family.

One day, the new Marquesa found the locked door and curiosity overtook her. She took a key that fitted the lock and entered the room to find the seven crystal coffins covered in dust and cobwebs, and behind the seven layers of glass, a girl dressed in rags. Inquisitiveness enticed her back, and on each visit she noticed the coffins were lengthening, and the raggedy child was growing. She reasoned this must be a spell cast by those infuriating fairies, the *Buffardello*, *Monachicchio* or *Scazzamurrieddhru*, and there might be gold hidden in the coffins.

She opened them one by one, yanked the ragged child out by the hair and accidentally knocked the comb free. Lisa's eyes flickered open, stared at the Marquesa, and she said, 'Mother?'

'Do you look like a daughter of mine?' said the Marquesa. 'Look at your rags, you are nothing, a mere artless peasant.'

She ordered her servants to cut Lisa's hair and scrub her scalp to remove the lice, and informed her she was now the property of the Marquis and the Marquesa and must do as they ordered. Lisa was given to the sharecroppers to help pick and dry tobacco in return for food twice a day and a bed amongst the straw in the barn. And each day, the Marquesa found a reason to beat her, until her mouth swelled like beetroot.

The sharecroppers were kind, and at night she sat round the fire while they spoke of their dreams of owning their own farms. They told the tale of a tenant farmer who ran away to the city where she sold homemade ice cream from a handcart. Her five sons struggled to keep the farm running without her and were in debt to the *padrone*, who offered to buy them a new slave girl, but they only wanted their mother. Later that day, an old woman dressed in rags and a headscarf came and told the boys she had bought the farm from the *padrone*, having made her fortune making ice cream for the city folk. The boys recognised their beautiful mother, and from that day the family kept every penny they earned and lived off homemade ice cream.

Lisa knew this was a dream, a fairy tale, and the sharecroppers would never own land because the Marquis only paid them in kind, never in money. Yet they spoke of nothing but his nobility and the beauty of the Marquesa. Lisa licked the blood from her lips and held her tongue at the thought of the Marquis's benevolence and his wife's bullying.

One day, the Marquis told the sharecroppers he was going to the town to collect some coffee beans he had imported, and he asked what gifts they would like. Some wanted coffee, others wine, books or clothes, until at last, he looked at Lisa, little knowing she was his rose-daughter. He took hold of her chin and turned her face this way and that, and for a moment he saw something – a spark, a light, a memory.

The Marquis asked, 'And what gift would you like, ragged girl?'

Lisa brushed his hand away, fixed his gaze, and through bruised lips said, 'Bring me a doll, a knife, and ice cream. Forget, and the river will stone you and drown you!'

The Marquis laughed at the impertinence of the child, and immediately forgot both his promise and the ragged girl's curse.

He was on his way home from town with his coffee beans and gifts for the *mezzadri* when he arrived at the river just as a storm blew. The waters churned, threw stones at him and threatened to drown him. He remembered the ragged girl's curse and realised he had forgotten her gifts. He returned to the town to buy a doll, a knife and ice cream, and when he approached the river, the storm calmed, the waters smoothed and he crossed with ease.

When he gave the gifts to Lisa, she snatched them, crawled under the kitchen table, sank her bruised lips into the ice cream, and held the limp ragdoll before her.

'Doll, speak to me.'

The doll stared through beady eyes into nothingness.

Lisa pricked her hand with the knife and wiped a drop of blood on the doll.

'Doll, be a friend to me.'

The doll swelled like a bagpipe, 'You won't have any need for friends if you lose all your blood. Here, let me.'

And the doll tore a rag from her dress and bound Lisa's hand.

'May I tell you my story?' asked Lisa.

'Is it short? I can't bear long dreary fairy tales.'

'It will take only one breath.'

'Go on. But let me lick your ice cream.'

The Marquis stood in the doorway, listening.

Lisa took a deep breath, 'I was born from a rose-leaf, my mother was a seamstress, my father a Marquis. A fairy cursed me, I was buried within seven crystal coffins, my mother died, the

Marquis enslaved me, the Marquesa beat me, and I lived, thanks to the kindness of the sharecroppers and the fairies. And now, I shall chop off the heads of the Marquis and the Marquesa!'

Lisa wiped the knife on her dress.

The doll was covered in ice cream, 'Beheading is too messy, honey. Show kindness, like the sharecroppers showed to you.'

'But the Marquis cares nothing for the sharecroppers, and his wife is cruel.'

The Marquis burst into the kitchen, and asked, 'You are my daughter?'

Lisa stared from beneath the table, and the Marquis suddenly remembered how much he loved to sit under tables when he was a boy.

He begged forgiveness, held out his hand, helped Lisa to her feet, and offered to marry her to make amends.

The doll finished the ice cream and spoke, 'You're already married, babe, and she's your daughter. That would be wrong. Very wrong!'

Lisa added, 'If you have truly changed, help the sharecroppers.'

So, the Marquis arranged a feast for the *mezzadri*, who sat at trestle tables while he served them imported coffee, wine from his vineyards, and homemade ice cream bought from an old woman's handcart in the city. And he bequeathed the farm to Lisa, who gave each sharecropper enough land to grow vines and make their own prosecco. For only a girl born of a rose understood the pain of thorns, and that sharecroppers, seamstresses and fairy-girls were one and the same.

So ends this tale of tales.

9

Sjökungen and the Troll Artist

SVERIGE, SWEDEN

E ster Ellqvist was born in Skåne in 1880 and raised as a social-
ite in Stockholm, where she attended the Royal Swedish
Academy of Arts, at that time split into male and female
colleges, which discouraged Ester from becoming the professional
artist she seemed destined to be. Instead, she met John Bauer, two
years younger and studying at the academy.

John was born into a farming family from Rogberga and was
schooled by Lake Rocksjön in Sjövik, Jönköping, on the south shore
of the sea-like Lake Vättern. His interest in folk culture was stimulated
by his first book commission, which involved travelling to Sápmi to
draw the nomadic culture and mythology of the Sámi for *Lappland,
det stora svenska framtidslandet*. In 1906, Ester and John married.

Between 1907 and 1916, John illustrated a set of folk tales for the
children's annual, *Bland Tomtar och Troll*, and his images of *tomte*
and trolls have defined the visual imagery of Swedish folklore ever
since, and inspired Jim Henson's films *Labyrinth* and *Dark Crystal*,
and Brian Froud's *Faery* books.

Soon, Ester and John were living their life as if it was a fairy tale.
They moved to Gränna, near John's birthplace on the banks of
Lake Vättern, to be near the forests he loved as a child and to raise
their son, Bengt. Ester was romanticised as his muse, a wild creature of the woods, and model for the golden-haired princesses who
appeared in so many of his illustrations, a fate so often bestowed on
the partners of famous male artists.

In the 1910 edition of *Bland Tomtar och Troll*, John illustrated
'*Agneta och Sjökungen*' ('Agneta and the King of the Lake'), a folk
tale retold from a woman's perspective by the Danish fairy-tale
writer and poet Helena Nyblom, and set by Lake Vättern. Ester was
John's model for Agneta.

On an island in the middle of the lake stood a red stone castle with a golden roof, the home of a wealthy man who called himself Sjökungen, the King of the Lake, though he was no mythical spirit of the water. His riches came from mining and gas extraction, he leased land to the military for shooting practice and felled the forest for house construction and to provide wood for the matchbox factories in Jönköping. But he had lost his wife and retreated into himself to escape his monsters, supported only by his daughter, Agneta, who loved her father but despised his work.

'Stop building so many houses, father, leave the forest to the birds and trolls. You'll have a heart attack!'

'Agneta, how will I pay for you to go art college? There's no money in painting unless you run a gallery.'

'I'll work in a bookshop and paint in my spare time.'

'Or find yourself a rich man to marry?'

'I am myself, father. No man will tame me.'

'I've noticed. And stop protesting about my logging businesses.'

Father and daughter fought like cats but respected each other's humanity.

One May Day eve, the scent of lime blossom filled the air and spirits walked the land. Agneta sat on the end of the jetty, wiggled her toes in the water, poured hot chocolate from her flask, opened her sketchbook and drew the swallows that flew overhead. She shook her head at the rows of log cabins her father had built on the opposite bank.

As the sun melted into the lake, Agneta heard a splash and a large fish flipped out of the water and landed on the jetty. Except it was no fish. Its fins were arms, its tail legs, it was a fish-man with a face coloured in shades of green, purple lips and eyes deep as the sea. Agneta picked up a rock.

'Touch me and I'll fry you for breakfast.'

The creature stared at her with the same sadness she recognised in her father and spoke with bubbling sounds.

'I don't understand fish-speak. Who are you?' asked Agneta.

It looked down.

'You live in the lake? With the char? What's it like down there?' asked Agneta.

The purple mouth moved, and she heard words, not through her ears, but in her head.

'The sun shines golden, and the moon paints the water silver and there is only the sound of colour.'

It looked at her in a way that said, 'Come and see'.

'I have lungs, not gills. I'd drown,' said Agneta.

The voice said, 'Use your imagination.'

It knelt down and touched her bare foot. She kicked it off.

'Hands!' said Agneta.

He looked at her with such loneliness that she plucked a sprig of lime blossom and offered it to him. As he stretched out his arm, he took her hand and dragged her into the depths before she had time to think of protesting.

The sun set golden, the moon lit the lake in silver, and all was silence.

When Agneta did not come home, her father assumed she was sabotaging his logging machinery or had tied herself to a tree to stop his road construction, but when he found her shoes on the jetty, he feared she had drowned.

Time passed and he missed their discussions and arguments. He was no longer Sjökungen without his princess.

When Agneta reached the lakebed, the sun shone golden, the moon painted the water silver, the lakebed swirled with colour, and fish flew overhead like birds. It was as beautiful as Fish-man had promised, and she could breathe, and she was angry.

'You brought me here against my will. That's abduction in my world. Please don't lay your hand on me again, or I'll make fish fingers of you.'

Fish-man examined his webbed hand, 'I wish you no harm. Yet your people catch mine with hooks and nets without a thought of abduction.'

She heard his voice clearly now, he spoke *Svenska*, and he seemed more human, in the way a native speaker is fluent in her own language yet awkward in others, or a seal is sleek when swimming but ungainly on land.

'You are Sjökungen?' she asked.

He explained. 'I am no King. I am the lake itself. I was once a great sea, but your people cleared the forests and built houses around me. I heard the cries of the tomte and trolls. Look around.'

Scattered on the lakebed was mining machinery, factory waste, discarded munitions from the shooting range, and shipwrecks full of human bones and seaweed. This was no utopia.

Sjökungen held out his webbed hand, 'Fish don't have fingers.'

Agneta realised time was not linear here. It lapped up and down with the tide and swirled around like shoals of fish. She had no memory of childhood, though she remembered she used to draw, but how could she have painted in watercolour down here? And whose children were those? Were they Sjökungen's? Or hers?

๑๖๑

In 1918, the Bauers' marriage was in difficulties. Amidst the food shortages and rationing caused by wartime blockades, John's illustration work had dried up and he was experimenting with large oil paintings and murals, while Ester missed her friends and family and longed to resurrect her painting career. They decided to leave, and on the evening of 19 November, a week after the war ended in Europe, they set off for Stockholm.

They were detoured following a train crash at Getå, which meant the first leg of the journey was across Lake Vättern on the steamer *Per Brahe* from Gränna. The cabins were packed, and the deck loaded with unsecured iron stoves, ploughshares, sewing machines and barrels. A storm gathered, the cargo broke free, and the ship listed in sight of the harbour at Hästholmen.

๑๖๑

Agneta was playing with her children when she heard the storm above the water.

She asked Sjökungen, 'Is that rain? How do I know that is rain? Is there land above the water? Do I have another family? A father? I must see him!'

Sjökungen had feared this moment.

He took her hand, they swam to the surface and hauled out like seals on the end of the jetty. Agneta shaded her eyes from the brightness. She smelled the lime blossom, swallows flew over her head, rows of wooden houses lined the lake, and the factories of Jönköping belched smoke. She saw a red stone castle, and memories poured into her head. An old man sat beneath a lime tree in the garden, drawing in a sketchbook, scribbles of trolls and *tomte*, and his eyes shone with the same sadness as Sjökungen's. He stared as if she was a ghost. It was May Day eve, just as it had been when she vanished.

A voice spoke in her head. 'Agneta, remember your children.'

The voice vanished into the water with a splash.

Agneta stayed with her father for a year, and when May Day eve came again, Sjökungen appeared, and Agneta remembered him and returned to her lake-children, and it felt as if only a day had passed since she left. On the lakebed lay the skeleton of an old steamer. She searched the deck and found a sketchbook filled with ink drawings of trolls and *tomte*.

Ester was 38 and John 36 when *Per Grahe* sank to the bottom of Lake Vättern with all the passengers trapped in their cabins. Newspapers suggested they had been taken by Sjökungen, the spirit John had illustrated for *Bland Tomtar och Troll* eight years earlier, and the Bauers would live forever in their fairy-tale land.

Agneta stayed with Sjökungen and her children for a year before returning to her father, and it felt as if she had only been away a day. Time was endless in Agneta's two worlds, so she could live with both of her *Sjökungar*. When she is on land, Sjökungen cares for the lake, and when she is below the water, the trolls protect the forests.

For what speculator or developer would dare argue with a troll?

10

Trolls

As John Bauer defined the visual mythology of Swedish folk tales, so did Theodor Kittelsen in Norway, who on hearing that a neighbouring illustrator was painting trolls, said, 'How can he draw a troll? He's never seen one!' Kittelsen illustrated trolls in his classic 1899 edition of *Norske Folkeeventyr* (*Norwegian Folktales*), written in 1845 by Oslo zoologist Peter Christen Asbjørnsen and theologian Jørgen Moe, who was later to become Bishop of Kristianssand.

Asbjørnsen and Moe met at school in Ringerike when they were 14, and inspired by their near contemporaries, the Grimms, they began collecting oral folk tales, which they retold using dialect words in the fledgling Norwegian written language. Their trolls were libertarian bullies, all brawn and little brain, who lurked around fjords, beneath mounds, behind trees and under bridges on the fjells, where they raided empty cottages, ate goats and did pretty much as they liked, at least until they were outwitted. Little wonder trolls became synonymous with Internet bullies and twisted ideas of freedom.

The Finnish illustrator, writer, and painter Tove Jansson drew trolls as a metaphor for the Nazi invasion of Scandinavia in her cartoons for the political magazine *Garm* during the Second World War. In 1945, she developed the troll into a more sympathetic character in her first book, *Småtrollen och den stora översvämningen* (*The Little Troll and the Great Flood*). Tove later renamed her characters *Mumintrollen,* although her publisher thought no one would know what a Moomin was, but everyone loved trolls.

The mountains and coniferous forests of Norway are made from trolls. Theodor Kittelsen often drew them as rocks and trees, an ancient people hidden in swamps and caves, trying to repel invaders from taking their land.

In a ditch beneath a wooden bridge on the Dovrefjell lived a great big troll with eyes the size of saucers and a nose as long as a poker. It was like an enormous moss-covered rock with an oak tree on top for hair and it smelled of rancid ditch water. It lived with more trolls, who might have been its children or grandparents but it didn't know because it wasn't bright, and anyway, it would probably all go wrong, because everything always did, because it was a troll.

The troll family were looking forward to *Jul* (Christmas), when they marched down from the Dovrefjell and went to Halvor's house to eat his food and drink his beer and party the day away, while he went to Trondheim to visit his sister. He was the only person who showed any kindness to the trolls. Everyone else thought they were rude, smelly beasts that liked breaking things.

On *Julaften*, Little Christmas Eve, Halvor was packing his bag when there was a knock on the door, and there stood a great white bear who asked for a bed for the night. Halvor explained that the trolls would arrive in the morning, and they stank of rancid ditch water. The bear said she could live with the troll smell in exchange for food, a warm fireside and a peg for her nose. So, Halvor made a bed for her by the stove, and laid the table with rice porridge, sausages, *sirupsnipper*, *smultringer*, *ingefærnøtter*, and troll-shaped *pepperkaker*, and gallons of *aquevitt* to prevent the trolls trashing the place in search of more.

The bear spent a peaceful night warm in a fug of steam that rose from her damp fur, only to be woken early the following morning as the trolls came down from their rancid ditch on the Dovrefjell, and stood outside the house dressed in their knitted Christmas sweaters, singing:

> Trolls are big, trolls are small,
> Trolls have long tails, some no tails at all
> Trolls have long, long noses
> Trolls have feet with long, long toeses,
> Trolls are bald and have big bellies
> Trolls are hairy and all are smellies.

They crashed through the door, danced round the tree, ate all the food, drank all the drink, and were about to look for more, when one of the little trolls spotted the white bear asleep under the stove.

'Hey, Halvor has a pussycat! Here, pussy, have a *pølse*,' and it shoved a half-eaten sausage on a fork under the bear's nose.

The white bear grumbled about being woken, growled, stood up, opened her mouth full of sharp white teeth, and bit the troll on the bottom. The little troll looked surprised, then burst into tears, and ran to its parents, crying like a child who's been told she can't watch any more TV.

The biggest troll stood in front of the white bear like a stone wall, oozing pondweed and slime, and stared through saucery eyes, dewdrops dripping from his long poker nose:

They call me Troll,
Gnawer of the Moon,
Giant of the Gale-blast,
Curse of the Rain-hall,
Companion of the Sibyl,
Night-roaming hag,
Swallower of the heavens,
For what is a Troll but that?

The bear laughed, 'That's from Snorri Sturluson's *Skáldskaparmál*, back when you trolls were noble people. Now look at you, you're overweight, you smell of rancid ditch water, and you're forced to hide away under bridges.'

The biggest troll realised this pussycat was stronger and smarter than he was, and she had very sharp teeth and even sharper claws, and everything was about to go wrong because it always did because he was troll, so he sat down by the hearth and said, 'May I tell you a story, Ms Pussycat?'

❧

'Once, we trolls lived on the slopes of the Dovrefjell, where we grew sweet grass that we made into hay for *julekake*, [Christmas bread]. We were happy, until one day, *tre bukkene bruse* [three billy goats], big as mountains with horns the size of moose antlers, tried to cross the bridge and take our fields. So, I thought very hard until I had an idea. I'd never had an idea before. It was a cunning idea. I hid in the ditch beneath the bridge and waited.

'"Trip, trap, trip!" said the bridge.

'"Who's that tramping over my bridge?" I roared from under the bridge.

'"*Den minste Bukken Bruse*," said the little goat. He wasn't little. He was the size of a hill.

'"Go away or I'll eat you," I said.

'"I'm too little to eat," said the billy goat, "I want the grass over the bridge."

'"That's my troll grass for *julekake*," I said.

'The little billy goat trip-trapped over the bridge, so I ate him up.

'"Trip, trap, trip!" said the bridge

'"Who's that, tramping over my bridge?" I growled.

'"*Den mellomste Bukken Bruse*." This goat was the size of a fjell.

'"Go away or I'll eat you like I ate the little billy goat," I said.

'"I'm too old and tough to eat," said the billy goat, "I want all the grass in the field over there."

'"That's my troll grass," I said.

'The middle billy goat trip-trapped over the bridge, so I gobbled him up too.

'"Trip, trap! Creak! trip, trap! Creak!" groaned the bridge.

'"What's that creaking over my bridge?" I trumped.

'"*Den store Bukken Bruse*." This one was BIG as a mountain.

'"Go away or I'll gobble you up," I said.

'"I eat trolls for breakfast," said the biggest billy goat, 'I'm the GGOAT. Greatest Goat Of All Time! And I want all the grass on the Dovrefjell,' and he pawed the ground, pointed his horns and charged, chanting:

Jeg har to horn som spyd,
Med dem skal jeg stikke ut øynene dine!
Jeg har to store kampesteiner,
Med dem skal jeg knuse både marg og ben!

[I have two spears, to poke your eyeballs out your ears, and I have
two curling horns to crush the marrow from your bones.]
'Next thing I remember was flying through the air thinking,
"Oh, not again," then I landed in the ditch, bones crushed, belly
squashed, covered from head to toes in rancid ditch water. From
that day, trolls had to leave our homeland and live in the ditches on
the Dovrefjell while the goats ate all our grass.'

Og snipp snapp snute, så er det eventyret ute.

[Snip, snap, this tale is done.]

The bear snored in the warmth of the fire, so the trolls tip-toed
out of Halvor's house with trolly-bags full of leftover food so they
could continue their Christmas party in the rancid ditch on the
Dovrefjell.

When Halvor came home after visiting his sister, he found his
cottage untrashed so he cooked the bear porridge and sausages, and
invited her to stay with him.

Next Christmas Eve, Halvor was in the forest cutting wood when
a voice spoke, 'Halvor?'

He looked round and there was the biggest of the big, smelly trolls trying to hide behind a tree.

'Have you still got your scary white pussycat?'

'She's waiting for you at home by the stove to tell her a story,' said Halvor, 'and she has seven kittens who are even bigger than she is.'

The Troll lumbered back to his rancid ditch to fetch his family, and they celebrated Christmas at Halvor's house with his pussycats, and he told the story of Kari Trestakk, who wore a wooden cloak and cured three trolls who gave her golden, silver and copper leaves and apples from their forests.

And then they sang:

Når trollmor har lagt sine elleve små troll,
og bundet dem fast i svansen.
da synger hun sakte for elleve små troll,
de vakreste ord hun kjenner;
Ho aj aj aj aj boff. Ho aj aj aj aj boff.
Ho aj aj aj aj boff, boff! Ho aj aj aj aj boff.

[When the troll mother has put her eleven little trolls to bed,
and tied their tails together,
she sings softly for her eleven little trolls,
with the most beautiful words she knows.]

All this happened a long time ago, and the trolls are still sat in their rancid ditch water on the Dovrefjell, forever looking forward to *Jul.*

Og snipp snapp snute, så er det eventyret ute.

11

Ulda Girl and Sámi Boy

Sámi artist John Savio was born in 1902 in Bugøyfjord and raised by his grandparents who were fisherfolk and reindeer herders in Vardø. John was 3 when his father drowned on Varangerfjord on his way to buy a coffin for his wife who had died from tuberculosis, an illness her son inherited. Inspired by Edvard Munch, Albrecht Durer and Japanese woodcut artists, he made prints of Sámi culture and folklore and sold them from door to door, though he never earned much and sometimes pawned his drawings to buy back later.

He died impoverished, aged 36. Yet he is now recognised as the Sámi artist who defines the visual mythology of the European Union's only official indigenous people.

Sápmi, the last wilderness in Europe, has boundaries that cross Finland, Sweden, Norway and Russia, and is home to some 20,000 people whose traditional way of life has brought them into conflict with their neighbours. Their land has been divided, languages and political systems imposed on them, and within living memory children were punished in school if they spoke Sámi, wore *gákti*, *joiked* or played drums. And now they face a proposal for an Arctic railway across Sápmi from Rovaniemi in Finland to Kirkenes in Norway, funded by EU, Russian and Chinese money, that will open the land to mining, windfarms and further logging, cut the reindeer migration tracks in two, and create a new border through old communities.

In 1904, Emilie Demant, a student at the Women's Academy of Art in Copenhagen, was travelling on an iron ore train with her sister through Swedish Sápmi when she fell into conversation with the storyteller and wolf hunter Johan Turi, who told her he wanted to write and illustrate a book about his people in their native language, Northern Sámi. Emilie offered to help, providing he taught her about his nomadic life.

Over the following three years, she learned Northern Sámi at the university in Copenhagen, before returning to Sápmi to live with Johan's brother in a mountain hut outside Kiruna. She photographed and sketched the way of life, taught herself ethnography, and in the autumn of 1908, spent two months helping Johan write his book. It was published two years later as *Muitalus Sámiid Birra* (*An Account of the Sámi*), the first book written in Northern Sámi about the lives and folklore of the herders and hunters.

In the spring of 1908, Emilie stayed with Anna Rasti of Karesuanto, who told her the story I retell here, along with another from Margreta Bengtsson, a mother and herder from Pite Sápmi. They are adapted from Barbara Sjoholm's 2019 translation of Emilie's *Sámi Folktales and Legends, a*nd feature the Ulda, the underground people, mountain spirits or miners, who lived as unseen as the Sámi, at least until *Frozen*'s Elsa and Anna became worldwide superstars.

A *siide* of Sámi reindeer herders arrived at a campsite in the northern mountains, when they discovered some of the herd had wandered off. A young Sámi boy was told to go and find them, so he tramped all the way back to the campsite they had just left, and there they were, nibbling at the moss through the snow. It was late now, and he was tired, so he decided to sleep inside the communal *goahti*, and re-join the herders at first light. He climbed inside a muslin tent to stop the mosquitoes biting and went to sleep.

He was woken by the sound of fingernails scratching on the muslin. He heard giggling, opened his eyes and saw the silhouettes of two figures. They looked like Ulda girls, which meant trouble. They were always looking for Sámi boys to take to Pohjola, the underworld, or so his mother told him.

The scratching stopped, and one of them spoke, 'Your turn, Áile.'

The shadow of another hand scratched the tent. He fumbled around for the needle he used for repairing leather, pricked at the hand through the muslin, and said, '*Jupmel*! Go away, let me sleep!'

'I can't,' said Áile, staring at her hand. 'I can see my blood.'

She told the other girl to tell the Ulda what had happened, and she sat in the doorway of the hut and licked at her wounds.

The boy couldn't sleep, so he left the tent. His mother had warned him that Ulda girls could enchant silly boys like him. Better to find a nice Sámi girl.

'What do you mean, you can't go home?' he asked.

'You've drawn my blood, you crazy man,' Áile spoke in a Sámi language that he could barely understand, 'When I see my blood, I become part human. My people won't let me back now you've pricked me.'

'Well, I had to prick you. My mother would have been angry if I hadn't. You were trying to drink my blood like a Stállu!'

'I don't drink blood. I eat *gumppus*, blood sausages. And Stállu are big and hairy. Do I look big and hairy? And my mother wouldn't like her daughter to be pricked by a crazy Sámi boy's great big needle!' she grinned.

'You're a rude girl. You should behave.'

Áile stared at him. He was handsome, but simple. 'Sit here, I'll tell you a story about the Ulda and the Sámi.'

'Okay, but don't burn my testicles.' Sámi boy sat down beside her.

'Ulda have lived here as long as Sámi, hidden beneath the mountains where the sun always shines. We keep cattle, sheep and goats, and mine for gold. We have feasts on trestle tables with flatbread, cloudberry jam and ice cream served on white plates with gold rims. We have smartphones that haven't been invented in your world of eternal cold and seasonal transhumance.

'One day, an Ulda girl met a Sámi hunter from Heahttá and they were crazy in love, but their blood was weak. He pricked her, and the old pipe-smoking woman appeared, the one who steals children and drinks blood. She cursed the girl to remain above ground with the Sámi, so the hunter threw his knife at her, but she vanished with enough blood to make *gumppus*.

'Ulda girl and Sámi boy travelled, lived off berries and nuts, and slept in holes in the ground, until one day she stared into his eyes and told him that no matter what he heard or saw, he was to stay in his hole for three days, then she would fetch him. He must trust her.

'In the hole, Sámi boy heard hammering and hollering followed by silences, and he thought the old woman had returned to drink his blood, but he stayed calm and trusted Ulda girl. After three days, he climbed out, and there stood a *goahti*, a great tent, a home made of wood and hide, with trestle tables laid with flatbread, cloudberries and ice cream. And their own herd of reindeer.

'She showed him how to lasso a reindeer cow and hold it firm while she milked it, and warned him not to swear, even if the reindeer kicked him. But it kicked him in the groin. "*Jupmel!*" and the poor reindeer dropped dead. It happened a second time, and wolves came to eat the reindeer. By the third time, he learned from his mistakes and kept silent.

'And that's how the Ulda taught the Sámi how to lasso reindeer, build houses, and never swear or joke when they work.'

Áile finished her story, and Sámi boy looked confused.

'Are you Russian?'

'I'm Ulda.'

'Inuit?'

'Ulda.'

'So, if I marry you, your people will build me a *goahti*, make me food and give me a herd of reindeer?'

Áile gave him a look, 'Ulda girls choose our own husbands, and only if we want one. Trust me. And no swearing! Can you do that?'

Sámi boy looked more confused, but he nodded, and crawled back into his tent, while Áile sat in the doorway of the hut and watched the northern sky.

In the morning, her friend returned with Áile's brother and their herd of reindeer. Her brother said that now she had been pricked by a Sámi boy, they must split their herd of reindeer and she could take half as her dowry.

Áile protested, 'I'm not married to him, he pricked me with a needle.'

Her brother grinned, 'I know what being pricked with a needle means. You're Sámi now.'

Áile whispered to Sámi boy, 'When you choose a reindeer for my dowry, catch the pretty ox-deer. He's a lucky charm, and my brother wants him, so hold firm. Trust me?'

Sámi boy nodded. When the herd was separated in two, he took hold of the ox-deer and clung on for dear life. Áile's brother was angry but kept his word.

Áile untied the harness on the ox-deer, and thanked Sámi boy for trusting her, and said they would always have good luck.

That evening Áile and Sámi boy sat in the doorway of the hut and watched the lights dance in the northern sky, and she told him another story.

'Ulda girl and Sámi boy were caught by a Stállu, a big hairy thing, crazy as a troll, who appeared before Christmas like a bad Santa. Stállu took them home and told his wife to drain their blood into glasses, make *gumppus* and roast the meat for Christmas dinner.

'"They're too skinny," said his wife. "Their blood won't make one sausage."

'Ulda girl said, "Mrs Stállu is right. We're too skinny to make a meal. Fatten us up with flatbread, cloudberry jam and ice cream, and you'll have a fine Christmas dinner."

'Stállu thought this was a good idea, so he locked the children in his shed and fed them every day to make them plump as chickens.

'Ulda girl gave Sámi boy a wishbone and whispered in his ear.

'At Christmas, Stállu came for his dinner and told Ulda girl to bare her breast. As he reached out his hairy hand, Sámi boy thrust the chicken bone into it.

'Stállu felt the bone, "You're still skinny. You won't fill my belly!"

'He threw the children away and they landed in the doorway of their hut, just like us. You see, Sámi and Ulda together bring good luck.'

From that day, Áile and her Sámi boy had good luck. The Ulda built them a *goahti*, brought them flatbread, cloudberry jam and ice cream. They protected the land from loggers and mining companies from over the borders, and every Christmas they left *gumppus* for Stállu, so he wouldn't drink their blood.

Which is very different to Christmas over the Finnish border in Rovaniemi, where visitors are greeted by an amusement park with husky rides that frighten the reindeer and ficti-tious stories about Sámi witches and Santa Claus.

12

Huldufólk and the Icelandic Bank Crash

ÍSLAND, ICELAND

At Tales Beyond Borders, a conference on fantasy fiction held at Leeds University in 2015, Alaric Hall, lecturer in the School of English and author of *Elves in Anglo-Saxon England*, spoke about the Huldufólk, the Icelandic little people. Dr Hall explained that following the bank collapse in 2008, people dealt with their financial issues by turning to the arts, folklore and creative writing, which inadvertently invigorated the tourist industry. People used to be attracted to the Icelandic Sagas, and now it's Elves, Bjork, Gabríela Friðriksdóttir, Katrín Jakobsdóttir and the films of Benedikt Erlingsson.

The Huldufólk have proved helpful in this transformation, especially with visitors who like to ask *Íslendingar* if they believe in Elves, which is rather like asking, 'Do you believe in Santa Claus?' They are also useful when speculators must be prevented from making unnecessary developments, a road project diverted, or a forest protected. They helped stop a road being built through the Alftanes Peninsula when the construction company were informed that the Huldufólk lived amongst the rocks on the proposed route. The Icelandic Road and Coastal Administration consulted their standard five-page guidelines, as the issue is so common.

At the same conference in Leeds, I gave a talk about the Tylwyth teg, who are quietly subverting environmentally unsound planning proposals in Wales, which also has a version of the tale below. Best not to mention names, though.

A poor farm at the foot of Eyjafjoll wasn't making any money, so the farmer told her husband that during the winter she would save

a few króna by spinning a bundle of wool into cloth to make a nice summer coat for him rather than buying one they couldn't afford.

Every day he asked if his coat was ready, and every day she replied, 'It will be when I've fed the hens, milked the cows, washed the pigs, cleaned the house, made your meals, brewed the beer, listened to your moaning, and …'

Later that day, an Álfar, an Elf lady, knocked on the door.

'Have you any work for a poor old woman?'

'Yes, spin this wool into cloth so I can make a coat for my husband and stop him moaning. I can't pay you much, though.'

The old lady laughed, threw the bag of wool on her back, and said, 'I'll be back on the first day of summer with the cloth, and all I ask in return is for you to tell me what my name is. You'll have three guesses.'

'What if I can't?' asked the woman

'That's for you to worry about,' said the Elf lady, and she cackled, did a little dance and vanished, as old ladies do in fairy tales all over the world.

When the winter snows passed, her husband asked for his coat, so she told him about the Elf lady. He said, 'She is one of the Huldufólk. She'll cook you up for dinner if you can't think of a name.'

'Okay, thanks, that's very helpful,' she replied sarcastically.

He added, 'Or she could be from the Dvergar or Jarðvergar [dwarfs or gnomes], maybe Ljósálfaror tívar [light-fairies or mountain spirits]. Either way she'll eat you.'

She told him to go and look after his sheep, while she sat by the fire with a bottle of home-brewed lava beer and searched for inspiration in her books of fairy tales. She found the story of Rumpelstiltskin in Germany, Ricden Rocden in France, Whuppity Stoorie in Scotland, Tom Tit Tot in England, Tucker Pfeffercorn and Ferradiddledumday in Appalachia, جعيدان or Joaidane in Arabic, Хламушка in Russia, and Sigl-di-gwt in Wales. It was all very interesting, but she couldn't pronounce these names, and this old Álfar lady was from *Ísland*, and probably had an Icelandic name.

She opened her book of *Íslenzk Æfintýri* (*Icelandic Fairy Tales*) by Jón Árnason and Magnús Grímsson from 1852. Jón was the first librarian of the National Library of Iceland, and Magnús was a student-turned-priest who included tales from his home in

Borgarfjörður. One was a story of a man who found a pile of seal-skins outside a cave where people were dancing, so he took one, and was followed home by a girl who wanted her skin back. She stayed for twelve years until she found her skin, and then she swam away with her children.

A selkie story, but she needed tales of Álfar and Huldufólk.

She found one.

Eve had so many children that she didn't have time enough to wash them all, so she hid the dirty ones away from God's watching eye. He told her not to have more children, and she said, 'Okay', but every year she bore another child, so she hid them beneath hills, behind rocks and in the forest, and when they grew up, they had children of their own, and they were the first Huldufólk.

Hmm, no names. She found another.

A traveller had lost his way, and after wandering about he came to a hut, knocked at the door, and asked an old woman if he could stay the night. She showed him to a warm room with two girls. He invited one of them to be his companion for the night. One girl agreed, and he asked permission to kiss her, and as his lips touched hers, his whole face sank through as if she was mist. She grinned like an Álfar and told him she was a daughter of those who refused to fight in the wars between Heaven and Hell. Instead, they hid in the rocks and mountains, and they were the first Huldufólk, who do neither good nor evil, and never hurt or abuse anyone.

The woman put down the book.

So, the Álfar wouldn't hurt her, but they might be troublesome, and she still needed a name. She drank some more lava beer.

That same day, her husband was up the mountain with his sheep, worrying about who would clean the farmyard and feed the chickens after his wife was eaten by the Elves, when he heard a voice. He followed the sound to a cave and there was an old Álfar lady sitting at a loom weaving cloth from his wool, and as the treadles clattered, she sang:

Hæ, hæ og hó, hó. Húsfreyja veit ei, hvað ég heiti
Hæ, hæ og hó, hó. Gilitrutt heit ég, hó, hó.
Gilitrutt heiti ég, hæ, hæ og hó, hó.'

[Ha! Ha! and Ho! Ho! The good wife doesn't know, Gilitrutt is my name.]

He wrote down the word Gilitrutt on a piece of paper in case he forgot it, and when he got home, he showed it to his wife, and told her what he had seen.

The woman wondered why she had not read this in Árnason and Grímsson. She opened the book and there it was. Gilitrutt. How had she missed it?

When the first day of summer came, the woman stayed in bed with a couple of lava beers and some homemade chocolates and waited for the Álfar.

When the old lady arrived with a bag of beautifully spun wool, she said, 'So, what's my name, eh?'

The woman nibbled a piece of *Íslenskt nammi*, 'Gabríela?'

'No!'

'Okay. Katrín?' said the woman, as she popped the whole chocolate in her mouth.

'No! Last chance,' and the Álfar dribbled and drooled.

'Okay. How about Gillý or Ruth? Perhaps both? Gilitrutt?' said the woman, taking a swig of beer.

The old lady gnashed her teeth and fell to the floor with a crash, as steam poured from her ears, green goo from her nose, then she got up and with what little dignity she had left, walked out without a word, never to be seen again.

The woman finished her chocolate and her lava beer and stitched the cloth into a coat for her husband. She named the yarn Gilitrutt and sold it for lots of money to the tourists who came looking for the Huldufólk.

'The cat in the vale, lost its tail, end of fairy tale. Okay?'

13

Otesánek and the Jeziňka Girls Who Steal Eyes

ČESKÁ REPUBLIKA, CZECH REPUBLIC

Back in college days I binge-watched the darkly weird short films of Czech animator and director Jan Svankmejer, along with his full-length *Alice in Wonderland*, complete with a stuffed white rabbit who escapes from a taxidermist. He followed these in 2000 with *Otesánek*, a live-action-animation of the Bohemian folk tale about a man and woman who raise a piece of wood as their child.

The story is rooted in fear of the monsters hidden in the dense forests, a metaphor for the ethnic conflicts between Czechs and Slovaks, and the Russian tanks that rolled into Alexander Dubček's socialist Prague in 1968 to quell the rebellion against one-party communist rule. Folkloric metaphor blossomed in fairy-tale films like *Valerie a týden divu*, which concealed its critique of politics, religion, authority and abuse of women within a dreamlike coming-of-age tale of a girl who just wanted a peaceful night's sleep.

These two tales of Otesánek and the Jeziňka girls are from *Slavonic Fairy Tales* by Karel Jaromír Erben, the archivist at the National Museum who collected oral Czech-language stories in Bohemia in the 1860s. My friend Nika was raised there over 100 years later during the Velvet Revolution, and knew these stories from childhood, and she says that despite all the nasties in Czech fairy tales, the Jeziňka aren't just nasty, they are the nightmares that lurk over the border between dream and reality. They are really, really nasty.

In a hut on the edge of a village close to the forest lived a poor man and a poor woman who herded sheep, built walls, dug holes, spun wool, darned socks, mended boots and took in laundry, anything to survive. If only they had a child, they thought, it would help them with their work. The neighbours said they didn't earn enough to feed themselves and the government wouldn't help, so how could they afford another mouth? But the man and the woman said they would go hungry to provide food for their little one.

One morning, the man was digging out tree stumps in the forest, when he found a small root with a head, body, arms, and legs. He hurried home with the root and showed it to his wife with a grin, 'Look, we have an Otesánek. A little boy of our own!'

The woman looked, 'It's a little girl.'

The man looked closer, 'No. He has a little twig. Look.'

The woman dressed the child in pyjamas, cradled him and sang a lullaby:

Spi, děťátko, spi!
Zavři očka svý,
Já tě budu kolébati,
Spi, děťátko, spi!

[Sleep baby sleep, close your little eyes, I will rock you bye, sleep baby sleep!]

Otesánek didn't go to sleep.

'Mother, give me food!'

She made porridge, Otesánek ate it all up, and grew a little rounder.

'Mother, more food!'

She said to her husband, 'You're right, it's a boy!'

She borrowed a loaf of bread from a neighbour, placed it on the table, and went to boil some water for soup. When she returned, Otesánek was sat on the table, big as a barrel, with breadcrumbs round his mouth.

'Mother, more food!'

'Otesánek!' she cried. 'Have you eaten all the bread?'

'Yes, mother,' answered Otesánek, 'I've eaten a bowl of porridge, and a loaf of bread, and now I'll eat you.'

And Otesánek opened his mouth and ate her up.

When the man returned home, he found Otesánek sat on the table, bigger than a barrel.

'Father, more food!'

'Otesánek? Where's your mother?'

'I ate her. I've eaten a bowl of porridge, a loaf of bread, and my mother, and now I'll eat you.'

And Otesánek opened his mouth and ate him up, and now he was big as a shed.

There was nothing left to eat, so he went to the village.

He met a little girl wheeling a barrow full of mushrooms.

'Look at you, Otesánek,' laughed the girl, 'You should eat mushrooms, they're less fattening.'

'I've eaten a bowl of porridge, a loaf of bread, my mother and father, and now I'll eat you.'

And Otesánek ate the girl, and the wheelbarrow, and now he was big as a barn.

Otesánek met a naked man chasing a pig with a curly tail.

'Get out of my way, tree-boy, I must catch my pig with a curly tail.'

'I've eaten a bowl of porridge, a loaf of bread, my mother and father, a girl with a wheelbarrow and the wheelbarrow too, and now I'll eat you.'

And Otesánek ate the naked man and his pig with a curly tail, and now he was big as an elephant.

Otesánek met a shepherd herding his sheep with his sheepdog, Vorish.

'You look like you've eaten a whole country, Otesánek,' said the shepherd.

'I've eaten a bowl of porridge, a loaf of bread, my mother and father, a girl with a wheelbarrow and the wheelbarrow too, a naked man and his pig with a curly tail, and now I'll eat you.'

And he ate the shepherd and all his sheep and his sheepdog, Vorish, and now he was big as Russia.

He was so full he felt he might burst, but he staggered on till he came to a forest where a Jeziňka girl was counting the eyes she had plucked from people's faces to stop them seeing what was at the end of their noses. Otesánek ate an eye.

'Stop eating my eyes, Otesánek,' said the Jeziňka, 'or I'll chop you up for firewood and fry your brains!'

'I've eaten a bowl of porridge, a loaf of bread, my mother and father, a girl with a wheelbarrow and the wheelbarrow too, a naked man and his pig with a curly tail, a shepherd and all his sheep and his sheepdog, Vorish, and now I'll eat you. And your eyes.'

The Jezinka wasn't afraid of a carnivorous tree, 'You are hairy on the outside, Otesánek. I am hairy on the inside.'

And she hit Otesánek with her axe and chopped him up for firewood, and out jumped the shepherd, sheep, sheepdog Vorish, naked man, pig with a curly tail, girl with a wheelbarrow, mother, father, bread and porridge.

And the Jezinka girl plucked out all their eyes and ate them with bread and porridge.

There are three Jezinka. They are sisters who live in the forest, and they are all very, very nasty.

The Jezinka girls were watching a poor orphan boy called Jeníček, who worked for an old blind man who lived in a hut on the edge of the forest. The old man told Jeníček to take the goats for a walk, and warned him, 'Be careful of the Jezinka, they will steal your eyes as they stole mine, and you won't be able to see what is in front of your nose.'

Jeníček led the goats into the forest, 'The Jezinka won't steal my eyes!'

The blind man thought, 'That's what I said before I went into the forest.'

Jeníček left the goats to graze and slept in the shade of a lime tree. The Jezinka stood over him. One touched his eyelid with a long red fingernail and carefully lifted it open. They licked their lips.

'He has juicy eyeballs,' said the eldest.

'They are blue as the sea,' said the second, dribbling.

'We can fry them up with his brains,' said the youngest, licking Jeníček's cheek with a rough red tongue.

Jeníček awoke to find a girl staring at him, dressed in white with a shock of jet-black hair. She held out her hand and balanced on the tips of her long red fingernails was a red apple.

'From my garden for you, look how red it is.'

Jeníček knew this was a Jezinky and the apple would make him sleepy.

'Thank you, but the apples are redder on my master's tree.'

'But my apple has no maggots. I ate them all. Your master's apples will have maggots, for sure,' said the Jeziňky.

'Thank you, but I want to keep my eyes.'

'You are a very nasty boy,' and she threw the apple at him and vanished.

Jeníček went back to sleep only to find another Jeziňky girl staring at him. She held a red rose in her hand and the thorns pierced her fingers.

'From my garden for you. Look how red it is, like the blood that drips from my hand. How sweet it smells. Here, sniff.'

Jeníček knew this was another Jeziňky and the rose would make him sleepy.

'Thank you, but the roses are redder in my master's garden.'

'But my rose has no thorns. I plucked them all out. With my teeth. Your master's thorns will scratch your white skin, and …' the Jeziňky dribbled.

'Thank you, but I want to keep my eyes.'

'You are a very nasty boy,' and she tore the petals from the rose and vanished.

Jeníček went back to sleep only to find a third girl staring at him. The youngest Jeziňky held out her hands and offered him a red comb. 'From my hair for you, look how red it is, like a deep cut. Let me comb you.'

Jeníček pulled up a briar rose and tied the girl's hands together.

The Jeziňky tried to move but she was rooted to the spot, 'Let me go. You have dandruff. You need combing.'

Jeníček bound her with more briars. She called for her Jeziňka sisters, and they told Jeníček, 'Release her, nasty boy, or we will pluck out your eyes.'

But Jeníček tied them all up with briar, rounded up his goats and rushed home to his master.

'He is so nasty,' said the oldest Jeziňky.

'Very nasty,' said the second, dribbling.

'He's fried my brain,' said the third.

Jeníček returned with his old blind master and said to the eldest girl, 'Give my master his eyes or I'll throw you in the river.'

'No, I had a bath last year,' cried the girl, 'I will give your master his eyes.'

The Jezinka led them to a cave with a large heap of eyes, great and small, red, blue, green and black. She pulled two from the heap and placed them in the old man's sockets.

'I see owls. These are not my eyes.'

'Oops, those were from a mouse,' said the eldest Jezinky.

Jeníček said to the second girl, 'Give my master his eyes, or I'll throw you in the river!'

'No, I like being smelly,' cried the girl. She pulled two eyes from the heap and placed them in the empty sockets.

'I see wolves. These are not my eyes.'

'Oops, they were from that little girl in red,' said the second Jezinky.

Jeníček said to the youngest, 'Give my master his eyes, or I'll throw you in the river!'

The Jezinky smiled and pulled two eyes out of the heap and placed them in the old man's sockets.

'I see fish. These are not my eyes.'

'Oops, those belonged to a seal pup,' and she pulled two more eyes from the very bottom of the heap.

The old man cried, 'I can see you, Jeníček. These are my eyes!'

Well, from that day on Jeníček and his master lived together, walked the goats and made cheese from the milk, and they could always see what was in front of their noses.

And the Jezinka girls watch and wait, for Jeníček has such tasty blue eyes.

14

Nita and the Vampir

ŘOMANI ĆHIB, ROMA

A long time ago, when the first Romany family left northern India to travel round the world, their wagon was so full of children tumbling over each other that their skinny old horse could hardly haul it. As it wobbled from side to side, the odd child was tossed into the mud on the rutted tracks. In daylight they could be picked up, but at night it was too dark to see. Those left behind put down roots and grew and had children of their own, and so the Romany came to be scattered around the Earth.

This tale was retold by Yefim Druts and Alexei Gessler, one a Russian poet and the other the son of a Moscow rabbi, and explains why the Romany people should be free to travel, for they share the same culture, stories and blood across the world.

In 2017, the council in Y Drenewydd, mid-Wales, invited the harpist Harriet Earis and myself to celebrate the life of the nineteenth-century Welsh Romany harper and storyteller John Roberts, who lived in a terraced house on Frolic Street and was famous enough to be known as '*Y Telynor Cymru*' (THE Welsh Harpist). John formed a family band with nine of his children and toured the country performing at theatres and stately homes, once for Queen Victoria, though on Sundays he could usually be found in the bar of the Bear Hotel or by the river entertaining the birds.

Harriet played many of John Roberts' tunes, learned from a largely oral family tradition through his great-granddaughter, Eldra. The project culminated in the unveiling of a blue plaque on a wall close to John Roberts' now-demolished home, to recognise the Romany in Wales.

John Roberts also told oral wonder tales learned from his Romany mother's family, and from his Welsh father's books of fairy tales. He wrote down some stories for the Gypsy scholar, Francis Hindes Groome, who published them in *Gypsy Folk Tales* in 1899 alongside a set of twelve oral Roma tales translated and collected by Dr Barbu

Constantinescu, the Romany-speaking son of a priest from Ploiesti City who became Dean of the Faculty of Theology in Bucharest.

The story here is retold from Constantinescu's *Probe de Limba si Literatura Taganilor din Româniaalong*, published in 1878. It reads as a metaphor for the demonisation of generations of Romany by people who have drained them of their culture and rights. It tells of a vampire who pre-dates Bram Stoker's Dracula, Bela Lugosi, Christopher Lee, Lestat, Angel, Eli the girl who asked to be let in, the Iranian woman who walks home alone at night, and the flat-sharing boys from the New Zealand shadows. It also mirrors the true tale of John Roberts' Welsh father, who had to fight for the hand of his Romany wife because her people wanted only strong blood to mix with theirs.

One evening, the young women gathered in the camp with their grandmothers to weave and spin, and the young boys came to kiss them, and soon everyone had partners, all except Nita. She was strong and clever, and had no interest in boys, preferring the company of her grandmother who told her stories. At least until a young *gorja* with silky black hair, sea-blue eyes and red lips came from the village. They kissed and he stayed until cockcrow, but when Nita awoke, he had vanished, as charismatic young men in fairy tales do.

Grandmother had been watching him, 'Nita, have you noticed anything about your young man?'

'No, grandma, only his sea-blue eyes,' and she flushed.

'*Chey*, he has cock's feet!'

Nita slept all that day and, in the evening, she took her sewing and returned to the grandmothers and the boys came and there was more kissing and love making, and her young man stayed till cockcrow and vanished.

Grandmother said, 'Nita, did you notice anything?'

'No, grandma, only his silky black hair.'

'*Chey*, he has horse's hooves for hands.'

Nita slept all that day and dreamed of men with chicken feet and horse's hooves. At night she returned to the sewing bee and there was more kissing, and her young man came and when he left at cockcrow, she stuck a threaded needle in his coat.

In the morning, after he vanished, Nita followed the thread to the churchyard, where she saw her lover standing in the shadow of a gravestone, his face glowing white in the moonlight. She went home to tell grandmother.

'Be careful, Nita,' said grandmother, 'your *gorja* thinks too much of himself. He will drain your lifeblood.'

That night he came again and asked grandmother, 'Where's Nita?'

Grandma stared at his cock's feet and horse's hooves and nodded to the other grandmothers, 'Nita's not here. Your blood is not for us!'

He said, 'My blood is strong. I will fight for her!'

He left, and the grandmothers agreed, 'He loves himself more than Nita. He will take our lives, as his people have always done.'

He went to Nita's *vardo*, and called, 'Nita, are you home?'

Nita answered, 'I am.'

'What did you see when you came to the churchyard today?'

'Nothing' said Nita.

'Tell me, or I will take your father.'

'I saw nothing.'

He returned to the graveyard.

In the morning, Nita's father had vanished. Nita and her mother searched for him, but he was nowhere to be found.

Next night her lover returned. 'Nita, tell me what you saw.'

'Nothing,' said Nita.

'Tell me, or I will take your mother.'

'I saw nothing.'

He returned to his grave.

When Nita awoke in the morning, her mother had vanished. She searched until her strength left her. She told grandmother, 'This man is draining me. If I die, bury me in the forest beneath the apple tree.'

That night he came, 'Nita, are you home?'

'I am.'

'Tell me what you saw in the churchyard, Nita, or I will take you, as I took your parents.'

'I saw nothing. You may take my life, but you will never take my soul.'

He returned to his grave.

In the morning, grandmother found Nita in her bed, drained of life. She was buried in the forest by the apple tree, as she had wished, and grandmother left herbs on her grave, and burned her few belongings.

The Zână, the fairies, watched over Nita's grave, where a blood red flower grew.

One day, the villagers were hunting with greyhounds and as they passed Nita's grave, the dogs smelled the flower, gathered round and howled. A Romany boy who was beating for the hunt pulled the dogs away and plucked the flower, took it to his wagon and placed it in a vase by his bed.

That night, while he slept, the flower climbed from the vase, stretched its leaves, turned head over heels and became a girl. She lay down beside the boy, wrapped her arms around him, kissed him and held him till dawn, when she returned to the vase, a flower again.

In the morning the boy told his parents of his strange dream, so his mother gave him a potion to help him sleep. That night flower-girl came again, lay with him in her arms, kissed him and held him till dawn, when she became a flower again. His shoulders were sore, and he didn't know whether he was awake or asleep, and he felt the life draining from him.

That night his mother and his father kept watch, and at dusk they saw flower-girl rise from the vase, and climb into their son's bed, and they recognised her. She was Nita. They tried to pull her from the bed, but the boy would not let her go. She lay in his arms till dawn and remained a girl, a flower no more.

The boy and Nita slept together each night and in time she gave birth to a dark-haired Romany boy.

All seemed well until Nita's old lover found her, the *gorja* who had drained her of life. He was a rich man now, he owned the village but it wasn't enough, he wanted more, as rich men do. He sold the land where the travellers were camped, so they were ordered to leave or he would set dogs on them.

He came to Nita, 'Tell me, Nita, what did you see in the church-yard that day?'

'I saw nothing.'

'Tell me truly, or I will take your husband, as I took you and your father and mother.'

'I have nothing to tell you.'

He returned to his grave.

In the morning her husband lay white beside her. Nita did not cry, she buried him in the churchyard, left herbs on his grave, and the Zână watched over him.

At night her old lover came again, and his lips were blood red, 'Tell me, Nita, what you saw that night?'

'Nothing.'

'Tell me, or I will take your child, as I took your father, your mother and your husband.'

'You will not take my child,' said Nita, 'I know what you are. You have stirred my blood and drained my people's lives, and now you are ready to burst.'

He grabbed Nita's arm, but she took a sharpened elder branch and plunged it into him, and he exploded, and the room was deep in blood. Nita cut out his heart and went to her husband's grave, dug him up, placed the heart on his chest, and he arose, as alive and well as before. And Nita went to the graves of her father and mother, and painted them with heart-blood, and they too arose.

Like Narcissus before him, the vampir desired his own reflection, and had gorged on his own lifeblood.

The vampir had taken their lives, but it could never own their Romany souls.

15

The Copper Man

УДМУРТИЯ, UDMURTIA

'Red is the colour of blood. Do not forget this.'

Think of redheads and the Scots and Irish come to mind, although there are many in Wales too, not surprisingly, given the shared ancestry, and also in Polynesia and amongst Māori in New Zealand. There are red-haired Tarim mummies in Xinjiang, a red-moustachioed iron-age corpse from Siberia, and the Egyptian King Ramesses II had red hair.

Henna and saffron were common hair dyes, and most bathroom cabinets have burgundy, auburn and copper colours in them, which makes it all the stranger that red-haired children used to be marked out as different, mocked and bullied at school, perhaps influenced by Aristotle's stereotypical view that redheads were 'emotionally un-housebroken'. Maybe non-redheads are just jealous.

The Udmurts of the oil-rich central Urals in Russia hold an annual Red Festival in Izhevsk to elect the reddest family, the most mischievous ginger child, and the copperiest goldfish. In the north of Udmurtia, near the silk road, people tend to be dark and Orthodox Russian, and work in the copper-smelting industry, iron foundries or weapons manufacturing, thanks to local man Mikhail Kalashnikov, inventor of the AK-47. While in the agricultural south, Udmurts are more red-haired and rooted in *vös*, the old faith. They see themselves as people of the forest, pacifists and polytheists who grow hemp, harvest timber, weave cloth, thread beads and brew *kumyshka*. In midwinter the water spirit, *vumurt*, swims up the Kama and Vyatka rivers from the land of the dead in search of mischief and marriage. This is the time for storytelling and riddling.

This tale, The Copper Man, is embellished from a collection of folk tales by the late nineteenth-century writer, poet and ethnographer Grigory Egorovich Vereshchagin, who produced the first

Udmurt Russian dictionary. The only available English version reads like Google Translate, so here is a rewrite – a parable about the urban rural divide and the effects of industrialisation.

Kátjá lived with her parents on a farm in the north of Udmurtia, close to the old Chinese trading route. Her father was an angry man who believed his family must speak only Russian, but her mother was from the south and followed the old ways. She wove cloth, strung necklaces of glass beads and taught her daughter to be *mush kad*, like a bee. Kátjá looked after the hives, spoke Udmurt to the bees and tied her mane of red hair round her waist to stop it dangling in the honeycomb.

At *vozo*-time, when the water spirits travelled upriver to visit their relatives, the farmer caught a Copper Man taking potatoes and flax from his fields. 'Curse these forest men! He'll be stealing my crops to make that evil liquor they drink. I will make an exhibition of him.'

The farmer threw the Copper Man in his barn, closed the little window, locked the door and left him to fester in the dark. He gave the keys to his wife, who placed them safely in her apron pocket, and he invited his friends and neighbours to see the strange little man.

The Copper Man stood on a bale of hay and looked out of a hole in the window, only to see a red-haired girl staring back at him. He called out, 'Please, help me?'

'You speak Udmurt?' said Kátjá.

'I'm a man of the forest,' said the Copper Man, 'I make copper kettles for brewing.'

'I'm Kátjá, a girl of the forest. I am *mush kad*. I'll help you.'

'You are like honey, Kátjá. I will pay you in wishes. Not in a fairy tale way. I'll be there when you are in need.'

'I'll fetch the keys,' and Kátjá was gone.

She found her mother churning cheese. Kátjá distracted her with talk of the bees, while her nimble fingers carefully lifted the keys from mother's apron pocket. She ran back to the barn and released the Copper Man, who took a thorn and made a little cut on his palm, and said, 'Red is the colour of blood. Do not forget this.' And he melted into the forest.

Kátjá returned the keys before her mother noticed they were missing, just as her father's friends poured down from the mountains in large wagons, each pulled by three stallions. They bustled into the barn, smoking their pipes, eager to see the Copper Man. But the barn was empty.

The farmer asked his wife where the keys were, and she pulled them from her pocket. He accused her of releasing the little man and raised his axe over her head. Kátjá stood in front of her mother and stared into her father's eyes, 'I released the Copper Man!'

The farmer lowered the axe. 'You red-haired women are crazy! You're all sorcerers, always sacrificing sheep to the dead. Go to Izhevsk and make Kalashnikovs instead of potions. Do your duty for Russia, or I'll cut off your hair.'

'My hair has red roots and will grow again,' said Kátjá as she wrapped herself in her shawl embroidered with the Tree of Life, gathered her few belongings and hugged her mother.

As she left the farm, she looked back to see her father chopping up her beehives. The bees swarmed angrily around his head and chased him until he jumped into the farm pond to escape the stings. Kátjá called to her children, and the bees flew after her as she walked away.

Kátjá walked south along the muddy roads towards Izhevsk, but the distant clatter of machinery and gunfire were not for her. She walked on towards her mother's land of forest spirits, where women stroked her red hair as a good luck charm and sang about Obyda, the girl who protected the bees. She came to Ludorvai, where the log houses tilted sideways and the villagers had left to work in the factories in Izhevsk, though a group of women had built a museum to the old way of life. One told her to go south to Karamas-Pelga, another said there would be too many tourists there, a third told her to visit Buranovo to see the singing *Babushki*, while a fourth said they were all stars now they had appeared on Eurovision.

Kátjá walked on until she came to a farmhouse with copper kettles strewn around the yard and the smell of *kumyshka* brewing.

She knocked on the door and it was opened by a tall boy with high cheekbones who was surprised to see a girl with golden bees swarming round her red head.

'I'm Kátjá,' she spoke in Udmurt, 'I'm looking for work. I'm strong and clever, I can milk the cows, harness the horses, plough the fields, and I'll build hives for my bees and sell the honey.'

'I'm Vasily, the farmer's son,' said the boy. 'This was an old Soviet collective, but there is no money in agriculture now. I'm leaving to make my fortune in the factories. You should speak to my father.'

Vasily introduced her to a smiling, stubble-chinned man who gave her a month to prove herself. So Kátjá herded the cattle, ploughed the fields, built new beehives, and the old farmer rubbed his sandpapery chin and offered her a share of the farm, on condition she solved a riddle.

He showed her three dozen rabbits in a big cage and told her to take them for a walk and bring them all back safely, but if she lost any … he drew his hand across his throat and made the sound of a knife slicing through flesh.

She opened the cage, arranged the rabbits in a line and ordered them to follow her, but they ran off in all directions, dug holes and made love, as rabbits do. She ran after them, flapping her arms until she was exhausted. She sang the song that called her bees, but the rabbits ignored her. She sat down by the stream and thought, 'I like bees better than rabbits!'

She licked a cut on her finger and remembered. 'Red is the colour of blood,' she said aloud.

'My old friend Kátjá. How can I help?' said the Copper Man.

Kátjá explained, 'I have to catch thirty-six rabbits and cage them so I can inherit a share in a farm, or my head will be cut off.'

The Copper Man smiled, 'Follow me.'

He led Kátjá along a stream, over a hill, and through a wood, until they came to a copper-coloured cottage. He opened the copper door and there on a copper table were copper plates stacked high with food, *perpecha* pizza, ear-bread, dumplings, pancakes, pastries, black bread, meat porridge and sour milk. There were copper kettles full of *peshchatem* and copper jars full of the most lethal *kumyshka*. The Copper Man told Kátjá to eat and drink her fill and all would be well. And he stuffed a large piece of copper cake into his mouth.

Kátjá ate till her belly ached, and she drank so much *kumyshka* that her head throbbed, and she resolved to tell the old farmer that she had lost all the rabbits, but who cares because bees are better than rabbits and, anyway, she can run the farm better than any man, so there and, and … she fell asleep.

The Copper Man woke her gently, wrapped a scarf round her neck and told her, 'When you remove this scarf, the rabbits will come to you. Wrap it round your neck and they will jump into the cage.'

Kátjá wobbled unsteadily back to the cage and removed the scarf, and sure as carrots are orange, all the rabbits came to her. And when she wrapped the scarf round her neck, they jumped into the cage.

Kátjá closed the door and returned to the farm, gave the rabbits to the farmer and before the effects of the *kumyshka* wore off, she told him, 'I am a girl of the forest, my hair the colour of blood. I will sell my honey and run this farm better than any man!'

The old farmer grinned and smelled her breath, 'Kátjá, you are strong and clever, and the Copper Man tells me you freed him from prison. My farm is yours! But don't drink so much, or you will spend all your profits!'

And so the old man retired. Kátjá ran the farm and her bees gave the most fragrant honey. Her mother left her cruel husband and came to live in the copper house where she wove cloth and made beaded necklaces, and at Christmas they went mumming from door to door, dressed in masks and old clothes, to welcome in the new year.

And at the Ižkar Festival, Kátjá was voted the most mischievous ginger.

'Red is the colour of blood.
Do not forget this.'

16

The Girl Who Became a Boy

SHQIPËRIA, ALBANIA

Twenty years ago, the Welsh photographer Rhodri Jones was sent by Oxfam to cross the Albanian border and document the changing culture following the death of Enver Hoxha and his brand of isolated communism. Jones' images from the northern mountains depicted a land of the living past, a poet's funeral, a swaddled baby, a sick entranced woman and the *vergjinesh*, young Lule and old Pashque, two women who had sworn to live in celibacy.

Jones followed in the footsteps of the writer, artist and anthropologist Edith Durham, who photographed and documented Albanian culture almost 100 years earlier. She was born into a wealthy London family in 1863, the daughter of an eminent surgeon, and while her sisters married or studied science, she attended the Royal Academy of Arts and became a natural history illustrator. Following her father's death in 1895, she looked after her sick mother, and became, in that telling phrase, unmarried in her thirties.

Freed by her mother's death, Durham cut her hair short and travelled through the Balkans on horseback, alone or with the Franciscan Padre Marko Shantoja of Okolo. She worked for humanitarian organisations, ran a hospital and refugee centre in Macedonia, documented the folklore and art of the mountain people through drawings and photographs, became close friends with the King of Montenegro, and reported on the Balkan Wars of 1912. She supported the newly independent Albania against Serbia, much to the displeasure of the British, who considered her eccentric, maybe a bit mad, although King Zog, who she also disliked, wrote of her, 'Albanians have never forgotten – and will never forget – this Englishwoman.' She became known as *Kralica e Malësorevet* (the Mountain Queen).

In her 1909 book *High Albania*, Durham described and photographed *burrnesha*, sworn virgins, women who voluntarily dressed as men to replace those killed in wars and blood feuds. In this way, they inherited farms or money, embraced celibacy, avoided

motherhood, escaped broken hearts and hid from the world in full view. She knew this story, written down in 1879 by the French diplomat, scholar and Albanian speaker Auguste Dozon, which explored the perceived boundaries between genders.

In a small town in Northern Albania, on the border with Kosovo, lived three sisters whose brothers had all died in blood feuds.

Eldest sister saw her father's sadness, and asked, 'What's wrong, father?'

He said, 'The king has enlisted soldiers to fight in the war, and I have no sons left.'

She said eagerly, 'I'll help. I'll marry a soldier and stand on the shoreline and await his safe return!'

Second sister added, 'I'll marry, too. Look, I have a pretty lace handkerchief to cry into.'

Youngest sister said, 'I'll cut my hair, wear a uniform over my red dress, take your sword, and fight to end the war.'

'You're a girl,' said her older sisters, 'You can't do that.'

Youngest sister pointed through the window at a man sat outside a café smoking a long *lula* pipe. 'That's Stana. His family lost all their men in a blood feud when he was a girl of eighteen, so she dressed in her brother's clothes, cut her hair short, and became a sworn virgin.'

Her two older sisters stopped her, 'You mustn't become a man. It would be embarrassing.'

Youngest sister pointed to a gnarled old man holding the reins of a donkey cart. 'Durdjan became a man after her parents arranged a marriage she didn't want. He worked in an office in Kosovo before he retired and came home. He told me he's been celibate for fifty years. I don't believe him, though.'

Her father said, 'Country girls become *burrnesha*, not educated ladies.'

Youngest sister was on a roll. 'Four brothers from a wealthy family in Tirana were executed for speaking out, so their educated sister became a man who supported his mother and earned his living writing politically charged travel books full of folk tales.'

'Stop,' said her father, 'Alright, you can be my eldest son.'

'I'll be neither son nor daughter. I'll be me,' and youngest sister cut her hair, filled her bag with sheep's cheese and walked over the old, covered bridge to enlist along with the young village men. No one recognised her, she was just one more soldier to be sent to the wars.

On the same day, a Kulshedra, a huge, multi-headed scaly serpent with breasts that dragged along the ground, came to town to eat all the children while the men were away. The king pleaded with Kulshedra to spare his people and offered his son instead. The townspeople watched as the boy was left alone in the town square while Kulshedra licked all her lips and opened one of her mouths to eat him. There was no *Dragùa*, no male hero to help, so youngest sister drew her sabre and chopped off one of Kulshedra's many heads, leaving a bloody mess on the town hall steps. Kulshedra picked up her head and stomped off.

The boy thanked her, 'My father will offer you land, but don't trust him. Ask for his horse. It can talk and is smarter than he is.'

The king offered her land, but she said, 'Thank you, I'm a traveller, I've no need for a home. My only wish is your country does not go to war.'

The king blustered, 'We must have war, or what will my soldiers do?'

'Then I'll have your horse instead.'

'Oh no, no, not my horse.'

The king's son intervened, 'This soldier saved me. Give him what he desires.'

The king was shamed in front of his people, so he gave his horse to this unusual soldier, who leapt onto its back, clung to its mane, and rode away.

The horse said, 'Good day, girl-dressed-as-a-boy. My name is Demirçil, and I will help you.'

'Ha, you are a smart horse. My name is Nora, but don't call me that when people can hear.'

'I will speak only when we are alone, Nora.'

They rode and rode and crossed the border into the land of the Mountain Queen, where a crowd of people gathered in front of the town.

Demirçil spoke, 'They are competing for the hand of the Queen's daughter, Illyria. Whoever jumps over the river and catches an apple will win her hand. I can jump the river if you catch the apple. You will like Illyria.'

The horse leapt over the river, and as it landed on the other side, apples were thrown by the crowd, Nora caught one and placed it in her pocket.

The Mountain Queen told Nora she could have her daughter, anything to be rid of the irritating girl who had developed a mind of her own and answered back.

'It would be your daughter's choice,' said Nora.

'She'll do as she's told,' said the Queen

'I won't,' said Illyria, 'but I like this soldier.'

That night Nora and Illyria went to bed, and weren't seen for three days.

The Mountain Queen's courtiers thought there was something fishy about all this and decided to be rid of this strange young man by sending him on an errand to the forest, where the Kulshedra would eat him for breakfast. Nora overheard and told her horse, who said, 'Ask the Queen for a cart and a team of oxen to pull it and leave the rest to me.'

On the way, Demirçil explained, 'When we get to the forest, Kulshedra will hear and come to eat you, but don't cut off another of her heads, yoke her to the cart in place of one of the oxen.'

When they reached the forest, Kulshedra recognised the soldier who had cut off her head and she had no wish to lose another, so she yoked herself into the ox cart and hauled Nora back to the town while the people cheered. That night Nora and Illyria slept together and weren't seen for a week.

The courtiers hatched another plan, to send this strange soldier on an errand to the well on the mountain where the wild mare would eat him for dinner. Nora overheard and her horse said, 'Ask the Queen for two pails of honey and a golden saddle and leave the rest to me.'

On the way, Demirçil explained, 'When we get to the mountain, pour two pails of honey into the well, climb up an overhanging tree with your golden saddle and wait. And don't worry, the wild mare is my mother.'

Nora did as the horse had told her. The wild mare arrived, drank the honeyed water, saw the golden saddle in the tree and said, 'What a beautiful saddle. I would wear it if only my son were here to see me.'

Demirçil galloped towards his mother as Nora dropped from the tree and placed the golden saddle on her, and the three of them rode through the town as the people cheered. Nora and Illyria weren't seen for a month.

The courtiers hatched a third plan, to send him on an errand to a church inhabited by snakes who never paid their taxes and would bite him to death. Nora's horse said, 'Ask the Queen for a wagon and two large handbells and leave the rest to me.'

On the way, Demirçil added, 'Climb through the window in the tower and ring the handbells. My mother and I will neigh as loudly as we can. The snakes won't like the noise and will be trapped inside, but be careful, they are tricky.'

So, Nora climbed through the window, rang the bells, the horses sang, and the snakes were so frightened by the noise they offered all their money to make it stop. Nora suspected a trick, and she was right. When the snakes saw the soldier, they said they would only deal with a woman who liked apples.

Nora took the apple from her pocket and removed her jacket and trousers to reveal her red dress. The snakes tried to wriggle out of the agreement, so the two horses neighed, and Nora rang the bells until the snakes gave them all their unpaid taxes to make them stop.

Nora and Demirçil hauled a wagon full of money through the town, and the people cheered. The Mountain Queen was so pleased, she offered to reward the girl in the red dress. Nora said, 'Redistribute this money amongst the poor, and give my horse and his wild mother a warm stable. I wish only for your daughter.'

The Mountain Queen said, 'Illyria is engaged to a soldier. You'll have to fight him.'

Nora dressed in her uniform, and said, 'There'll be no fighting. I'm the soldier, the Mountain Queen's daughter's lover.'

And Nora and Illyria went to bed, and as far as I know, they're still there.

17

The Hidden People of Anatolia

ANATOLIA, ANADOLU

In Kapadokya, Anatolia, there are two worlds, one lit by moonlight above ground, the other illuminated by candlelight below. On the surface are what the tourist industry calls 'fairy chimneys', natural rock projections carved into houses, while beneath the ground are underground cities like Derinkuyu, built in the Byzantine era around 1,500 years ago on existing cave formations. There are networks of subterranean caverns eleven storeys deep with narrow passages connecting the floors, designed to entrap invaders. Once, it housed up to 20,000 people, mostly Muslim Arabs escaping the wars, and has since been occupied by Christians, Cappadocian Greeks and refugees escaping further conflicts and persecutions.

Near Sivrihisar in mid-thirteenth century Anatolia lived the turbanned trickster, farmer, preacher, comedian, judge, imam, wise man and fool, Nasreddin Hodja, the one-eyed man who was king of the country of the blind. The village of his birth, Hortu, is now named after him, Nasrettinhoca, and there are countless stories about him, many of which he told himself.

Someone had stolen the Hodja's quilt, but instead of buying a new one, he bought a bow and arrow to protect himself and his wife Fatima from future robbers. That night, he heard a noise, and looked out the window only to see a shadowy figure lurking by the apricot tree in his backyard, cloak flapping in the wind. This must be the thief, he thought, perhaps some monstrous creature from the underworld, a shapeshifting djinn or gruesome ghoul, or worse, a poor man trying to rob him of his gold.

He told Fatima as she snored in bed, 'Don't worry, my dear, your noble Hodja will protect both you and our belongings.'

He threw open the window and told the thief, 'Return my quilt, or else.'

There was no answer.

The Hodja puffed out his chest, picked up his brand-new bow, loaded an arrow, closed his eyes and fired. He heard a thunk and saw the arrow sticking out of the figure by the apricot tree, and it dawned on him that he had shot a man. He dropped the bow, locked the window, climbed into bed next to Fatima and pulled the quilt over his head.

The quilt!

It was on the bed all the time.

And he had just shot the man who hadn't stolen it.

He lay there, trembling, until morning when, fearing the worst, he looked out of the window to see his best cloak, which Fatima had washed and hung out to dry, impaled to the apricot tree.

'You crazy man!' shouted Fatima as she pulled out the arrow, ripping the cloak even more, 'You could have killed someone.'

The Hodja smiled, 'Be grateful I wasn't wearing it, my dear, or I would have killed myself, and your dear Hodja would be dead, and then who would protect you from the demons of the otherworld?'

☙❧

That was 700 years ago, but time is an illusion amidst the fairy-tale landscape of Kapadokya. In March 2020, my friend Sitki had finished a PhD in international politics in Wales and was about to begin a new life in London. Just before he left, he told me the outline of this story.

In the early 2000s, Sitki lived with his mother, father, aunt and sister in a large four-storey house in Kapadokya on the road to Ankara. The house was on the edge of an old town, where the rows of red-roofed houses were so unsafe and damp they were due to be demolished and replaced with high-rise social housing.

The little brother and sister were scared of the long, dark corridors that connected the rooms in their old house, so whenever they needed to go to the toilet, they always went together. There were fairies and giants and ogres out there. They knew this because father had told them. In fact, he had seen them. They were as big as people, dressed in white with pale faces like ghosts. And what's more, they were seen in many of the old, red-roofed houses of the town.

Father said they were djinns and they lived all over old Kapadokya, lurking in quiet dark places like Aşağı Mahalle. They could be handsome men or tall *peri*-women with long shiny hair and voices that lured the impressionable to follow them to paradise or hell. They appeared on dusty roads on hot summer days, silently and suddenly in front of you, then behind, sometimes swirling like a whirlwind. Some said it was hot air that caused vortexes or dust devils, but most knew it was the Cin Düğün, the weddings of the djinn girls who whirled round like *Sufi*, until someone shouted aloud, 'Djinn, we can see you!'

The children's aunt told their father he was seeing things or making up stories to scare everyone, and he should stop. He had frightened her as a child with his scary stories, too, so perhaps this was time to get her own back. One evening, she dressed herself in white, rubbed flour into her face, hid in a corridor and prepared to terrify him.

That evening, father saw his sister hiding in the corridor, dressed in white, with flour on her face, so he crept up behind her and placed his arms around her. She didn't scream or jump, she turned round slowly and stared him in the face. And then a cold hand clutched his belly. It wasn't his sister. It was someone else, and they were flesh and blood. Father let go and the two figures separated and went their ways without a word.

Not long after this encounter, the family moved out and the house was demolished along with all the rest of the old, red-roofed buildings. A new concrete brutalist block was constructed, and some of the people who had been evicted from the old housing moved in. And every now and again, on a dark evening, figures dressed in white with pale faces would be glimpsed in the corridors and stairwells of the new blocks.

Maybe they were ghosts or djinn or *peri* from the old Persian and Turkish folk tales, or *karankoncolos* demons from Anatolian folklore, or perhaps they were Christians or Greek visitors from ancient Kapadokya, or a memory of when people were nomadic, searching for their ancient homes beneath the concrete and tarmac. Father believed they were physically real, impoverished people, homeless, out of work, living their lives unseen by their wealthier neighbours, a hidden underclass emerging at night, pale from lack of sunlight, living by the light of the moon. For it's true, we don't always notice those who have nothing, even if they stand right in front of our noses.

The Hodja once saw the reflection of the moon at the bottom of the well, and thought, 'The moon shouldn't be hidden away down there in the dark. It should be up in the sky, shining brightly for all to see.' So, he decided to return the moon to its rightful place. He tied a grappling hook to a rope, lowered it down the well and pulled till he thought he'd hooked the moon. But the hook was caught in the stone wall, so he pulled and pulled until it broke free, then he fell backwards and landed on the ground on his backside, with his belly in the air, looking up at the night sky with the moon shining brightly.

'There,' he grinned, 'now I have returned the moon from the darkness to its rightful place in the sky, where it will shine brightly enough to prevent me shooting arrows at men who hadn't stolen anything.'

18

The Bewitched Camel

سوریای, SYRIA

T he tales told by Scheherazade in *Les mille et une nuits* (*The One Thousand and One Nights*) were first translated from Arabic manuscripts by the French archaeologist Antoine Galland and published between 1704 and 1717. Galland was heavily influenced by the French literary fairy tales of Charles Perrault and Madame D'Aulnoy, until, in 1709, he met Antun Yusuf Hanna Diyab, a young Maronite Christian writer and storyteller from Aleppo in Ottoman Syria, who was studying in Paris.

Diyab wrote down seventeen oral folk tales in Arabic, including 'Aladdin', 'Ali Baba', 'The Ebony Horse' and 'Prince Ahmed and the Fairy Perī-Bānū', which Galland published in later volumes of *Arabian Nights Entertainments*. Diyab was never credited for his stories and returned to Aleppo, where he married, had many children and became a prosperous cloth merchant, the forgotten voice behind Scheherazade.

In 1926, German filmmaker Lotte Reiniger became the new voice of Scheherazade when she made a stop-frame silhouette-animated film, *Die Abenteuer des Prinzen Achmed*, based on Diyab's stories of Prince Ahmed and Aladdin. The original film was destroyed during a grenade attack on her Potsdam studio after she fled to England. However, a copy was found at the British Film Institute in London, restored and hand-tinted, making it the oldest surviving full-length animated film, eleven years before Disney's *Snow White*.

I toured Reiniger's film around the country a few years ago with a live soundtrack by multi-instrumentalists Ailsa Mair Hughes and Pixy Tom Owen, just at the time civil war and forced migration left Syrian people in search of new homelands. This tale was told in 2015 by Mahmoud Fares of Khan el Sheikh Palestinian Camp 7, and is adapted from *Timeless Tales Told by Syrian Refugees,* a collection of stories adapted to reflect their changing times. It is not a metaphor for conflict or displacement, but a story of power and injustice, an escapist entertainment about the two worlds of rich and poor, with a king as the butt of the joke, like so many of Scheherazade's *Thousand and One Tales*. And I've added a snippet from Prince Ahmed, in honour of Diyab.

A poor woodcutter had chopped up a log in the forest and was wondering how to carry it to market to sell, when he saw a camel wandering around lost. He tied the log to its back, went to market, sold the log, thanked the camel for its help, took it home, fed it some barley and gave it a place to sleep.

In the morning, he was surprised to find the camel had laid a golden egg. Same the following day, and every day, until the woodcutter wasn't so poor.

One day the woodcutter and the camel were in town when the chief merchant announced that all men must leave the market because Latifa, the king's daughter, wanted to visit the shops and didn't want poor people watching her. So, the woodcutter tied his camel in front of a shop and hid. The camel watched the king's daughter walk past and felt his heart flutter.

When they got home, the camel refused food and drink, and the following morning there was no golden egg. The woodcutter took the camel for a walk to cheer him up, but as they passed the king's palace, the camel wouldn't move.

'What's wrong with you, camel?'

'I'm in love.'

'Who with?'

'Latifa, the king's daughter.'

'You can't be. You're a camel.'

'I'll be miserable unless I can marry her,' and he repeated Latifa's name.

The woodcutter went to the palace to ask the king for his daughter's hand.

The king laughed, 'Why would Latifa marry a common tradesman?'

'I don't want to marry her. My camel does.'

Well, the king laughed till his belly near burst, and when he composed himself, he said, 'In the morning, bring me a never-ending bunch of grapes that I can eat forever, then maybe your camel can ask my daughter to marry him. When she says no, I'll have you and your camel beheaded.'

The woodcutter went home and told the camel that the king was going to cut their heads off.

'Don't worry,' said the camel. 'Go to sleep. All will be well in the morning.'

When the woodcutter awoke, he found the camel had laid a golden plate and fresh grapes. He took them to the king, who ate a grape, and another one appeared. No matter how many he ate, there were still the same number.

The king stroked his beard and said, 'Bring me a carpet that will cover the palace floors and the city street. Or …' And he drew his finger across his throat.

The woodcutter told the camel what the king had said.

'Don't worry,' said the camel.

In the morning, the camel laid a golden chest containing an enormous carpet. The woodcutter showed it to the king, who opened the lid, and, to his surprise, the carpet spread all over the palace and the city streets by itself.

The king was not one to look a gift-camel in the mouth, 'Build me a golden palace on the empty plot of land next door, so tall that it reaches to the clouds, and with a golden toilet.' He grinned like a lion waiting for breakfast.

The woodcutter told the camel what the king had said.

'Don't worry,' said the camel.

But the woodcutter did worry. This was impossible. Rich kings were unpredictable, and he preferred his head where it was – on his shoulders.

In the morning, the camel laid a glorious golden palace that hadn't been there the night before, right next to the king's old palace.

This time the camel went to see the king.

'Does it have a golden toilet?' asked the king.

The camel nodded.

'You are a camel who can make gold?'

The camel nodded again, 'I am Scheherazade's camel. Listen.

'A pompous and greedy Sultan had three sons, Houssain, Ali and Ahmed, and they all wanted to marry the beautiful Princess Nouronnihar. So, the Sultan arranged an archery competition, and whoever shot his arrow the furthest could ask for the princess's hand.

'Ahmed fired furthest but couldn't find where his arrow had landed, so Nouronnihar married Ali.

'Ahmed was still looking for his arrow when he found a cave and an underground stone house, the home of the mysterious djinn-girl, Perī-Bānū, who took him into her own bed. When the Sultan discovered that Ahmed was living with a rich djinn-girl, he decided to steal her wealth and magic, because he didn't think he was rich enough already.

'He set Ahmed three tasks, and Perī-Bānū easily solved the first two. The Sultan's third wish was for a mighty warrior a foot and a half high, with a thirty-foot-long beard and the strength to carry a five hundredweight iron bar on his shoulders which he used as a quarterstaff.

'Perī-Bānū sent her small, immensely strong but violently unpredictable brother, Schaiber, to the Sultan, who was so offended by the rich man's greed, he tore him into pieces.'

The camel added, 'So you see, King, that's what happens when rich and powerful men don't allow their daughters to marry handsome wealthy camels.'

'Alright, camel, marry my daughter,' said the king, hearing the word 'wealthy'.

Latifa hadn't been asked her opinion, 'Father, I will decide who or whether I marry. Although this camel is smart, and he lays gold. I'll have him!'

So Latifa the king's daughter took the woodcutter's camel to her bed.

And you might be wondering. Why? How? Well, Latifa was as smart as Scheherazade, and she suspected this was a bewitched camel that became a man at night. She was right, and their relationship had none of the problems that human ones do, although her sisters complained their brother-in-law smelled like a dung heap and snorted at them. Which he did.

One day, the king declared war on a neighbouring kingdom because he wanted more land, and the camel was called up to carry provisions to the front alongside all the other dispensables. Latifa made him a camel-coloured uniform to wear by night, and she swore to keep his secret for fear he would remain a camel forever.

One night, he was wounded and the king wrapped the injured leg in a handkerchief embroidered with the royal seal. He returned home before sunrise and Latifa bathed the wound before he turned back into a camel.

Later that day, her sisters were boasting that all their husbands had noble war wounds like shellshock, gangrenous legs and brain damage, while all her camel had done in the war was to be a camel. Without thinking, she told them he had fought alongside the king and showed them the bloodied handkerchief.

When the camel learned that his lover had revealed his secret, he sang:

An apple for the dove, an apple for the pigeon
And an apple for my wife who didn't keep my secret.

And he vanished.

Latifa wanted her husband back, so she built a Hammam in the market and offered a free bath to anyone who could tell a good story, especially if it concerned a camel. News spread and people came for their annual baths, and the air smelled so much sweeter.

One day, a poor woman who hadn't had a bath in years, packed her soap and a towel and headed to the city. She slept the night in a tree and had just settled herself down when the earth split open and a camel emerged, turned into a young man and sang:

An apple for the dove, an apple for the pigeon
And an apple for my wife who didn't keep my secret.

He sang until first light and then the earth opened, and he disappeared.

When the woman reached the city, she told the story to Latifa and spent the day scrubbing grime from her body. Latifa ran to the tree, climbed to the top and waited. When twilight came, the earth split open, her camel appeared, turned into her man and sang:

> An apple for the dove, an apple for the pigeon
> And an apple for my wife who didn't keep my secret.

She jumped on him from the tree and held on tightly all night long until the earth closed, and the curse was broken.

But the witch who had enchanted him was angry and set Latifa three tasks: to clean her house with a beaded broom, to carry a heavy chest to her sister, and to dance with happiness when the witch and the camel married. And if you want to know how Latifa carried out the tasks, read *Timeless Tales*, because your storyteller needs a drink.

I'll just tell you that Latifa and her camel-husband raised many children, and some of them were girls like their mother, some were camels like their father, but most of them were unsure what they were.

And there we are. Why should I keep my stories to myself?

19

A Tale From the Tamarind Tree: The Djinn Girl

SENEGAAL, SENEGAL

Senegalese *griot*, storyteller and musician Seckou Keita has recently collaborated with the Welsh harpist Catrin Finch to explore ideas of migration through music. Their latest recording, *Soar*, follows the flight of ospreys who winter in Senegal and fly across invisible human boundaries to breed in Wales, for birds have no need of passports. The master *griot* plays Ceredigion harp tunes on the twenty-one-string *kora*, and the harper replies with Senegalese rhythms as two musical languages weave in conversation.

Jali Mady Sissoko, known as Wuleng, the Red, was a flamboyant Wolof *griot*, from southern Senegal, in the early 1800s. One day, he was walking through the bush in Guinea-Bissau when he heard music so beautiful it sounded like the Mandinka language. Hidden in a hole in the ground was a djinn, a West African spirit, playing a twenty-two-string *kora*. The djinn helped Jali Mady become a *griot* to the warlord Kelefa Saane, and he walked from village to village with his *kora* stuffed down his baggy trousers.

When Kelefa was killed in battle, Jali Mady wrote a tune for him, and soon all the warlords wanted a *griot* with a twenty-two-string *kora* that spoke Mandinka. When Jali Mady died, his fellow *griots* removed one string from their instruments in his honour, but at home in southern Senegal, his twenty-two-string *kora* is still played beneath the tamarind tree, where stories grow like leaves.

One hundred years later, in 1906, Birago Diop was born in Ouakam. He studied veterinary science in Toulouse, worked as a vet in Dakar, and on independence became Senegal's Ambassador to Tunisia, all the while roaming the west African bush in search of folk tales.

In 1947, he published *Les Contes d'Amadou Koumba*, followed by a second volume in 1960. These were collections of tales heard on his travels, retold under the invented persona of his family *griot*,

Amadou Koumba. Diop wrote in French rather than Mandinka, but his stories carry the memories and wisdom of the Wolof people, featuring the animal tales of 'Leuk Hare', 'Bouki Hyena', 'Golo Monkey', 'Maman Caiman', 'Gaïndé Lion' and the supernatural Djinn-girls, who know how to fly over borders.

Look up from beneath the tamarind tree and you will see darkness, for the leaves are so thick they keep out the light, but look closer, and you will see the stars. Listen, and you might hear the *kora* speaking Mandinka, and you may see the djinn, but don't speak badly of them. One woman poured hot water on them to clear them out of the tree, and now she speaks to herself and howls at the moon.

One day, Koumba and her husband Momar sat in the shade of the tamarind tree, for they had never offended the djinn. Momar snored, while Koumba sewed and sang a lullaby to her lost child:

Woy wéét, woy wéét
Woy wéét adduna
Sama doom dem nii

[Lonely, lonely, lonely in this life, my child has gone away]

A voice spoke from the tree, 'Koumba, are you happy?'

Koumba looked up, and there, sat on the first branch, was an old woman with cotton-white hair pouring down her back. 'Yes, Mame,' replied Koumba. 'I have lost my child, I have a hump on my back, my husband Momar loves his second wife Khary more than me, and my sister was eaten by a vulture, but I am happy.'

'You have a good heart, Koumba,' said the old woman. 'I will gift you. Friday is the full moon, wait till you see the stars shine through the tamarind tree, follow the osprey towards the beat of the *sabar* to where the djinn-girls dance on N'Guew, the clay hill. Wait till ten dancers have joined the circle, then sing to the djinn-girl next to you, "*Aayo beeyo beeyo!*" and say, "Here, take this child from my back".'

And she vanished, as old women in fairy tales everywhere do.

When Friday came, Koumba wrapped herself in her kaftan, sat beneath the tamarind tree and looked up to see the stars shining through the leaves. She followed the osprey to the clay hill, heard the beat of the *sabar* and saw the djinn-girls dancing the *sa-n'diaye*, spinning around in the middle of the circle. Koumba clapped her hands to the whirl of the dancing.

One, two, three, ten had danced and ten had taken their places, so Koumba sang to the next girl, '*Aayo beeyo beeyo!*' and said, 'Here, take this child from my back'.

The djinn-girl took Koumba's hump from her back, just as the rooster crowed and the dancers vanished. Koumba ran back to her hut and stood up straight. Her neck was long like a gazelle, her braided hair tumbled down her back like a swallow's tail and her hump had gone.

In the morning, when Momar saw Koumba drawing water from the well with her straight back, he thought she was the most beautiful woman he had ever seen, so fickle are men. But his second wife Khary was as bitter as a Sinjan root.

Khary dropped to her knees and beat the ground with her fists, 'Koumba, help me get rid of my hump!'

'You don't have a hump,' said Koumba, 'You're beautiful as you are.'

'Yes, but my back will be straighter, my hair longer than yours, and Momar will love me more than you, and I will fly free as an osprey.'

Koumba thought, 'Hmm, he'll still see your green eyes!'

So Koumba told Khary all about the old cotton-haired woman in the tamarind tree and the djinn-girls on the hill. 'Be careful, Khary, don't be greedy, or Maman Caiman will eat you up!'

On the next full moon, Khary sat beneath the tamarind tree and waited till she saw the stars through the leaves and followed the osprey up the clay hill to the djinn-girls. She clapped to the rhythm of the dancing, one, two, three, ten, and Khary sang to the next girl, '*Aayo beeyo beeyo!*' and said, 'Here, take this child from my back.'

The djinn-girl said, 'No, not till the chickens grow teeth. Here, you take this child from me, someone left it on my back and it's heavy.' And she took Koumba's hump and placed it on Khary's back, just as the rooster crowed and the djinn-girls disappeared. Khary sat alone on the clay hill with two humps on her back. No one had ever noticed her hump before, and now she had two humps the size of mountains. She wept and wailed and ran through the night as if Maman Caiman was after her. She ran so far and so fast she threw herself into the sky and flew like a bird over the ocean to a faraway land where she built a nest for the two babies on her back.

Near where the ospreys breed in West Wales is another hill, Trichrug, close to where the harper Catrin Finch was born in Ceredigion, and where a young man called John the Painter was drawn into a circle of women dancing and played his flute for the Tylwyth teg, the Welsh djinn.

There are many versions of the story of the fairies and the hunchback, particularly from France. A Breton ploughman, Bénéad Guilcher of Morbihan, danced with the Korrigan, who removed his hump. An old miser called Perr Balibouzouk heard of this and asked the Korrigan to take his hump, but they played a trick and gave him Bénéad's instead. I wonder whether Birago Diop heard this French story when he was studying to be a vet in Toulouse, and told it to his imaginary griot, Amadou Koumba. For it only takes one bird to fly over invisible boundaries for a story to travel to another land.

Aayo beeyo beeyo.

20

The Hare and the Tortoise
(But Not That Tale)

MORIS, MAURITIUS

Katībuge Ibrahīm Saīdu, of Diguvāndo in the Maldives, told an old folk tale about a group of Maldivians in the seventeenth century who were sailing a twelve-oared *dōni* from Fuvahmulah when they were caught in a storm and washed up on the archipelago now known as the Chagos Islands, close to Mauritius. The stranded people had no tools to repair their wrecked boat, and the forests were dark and there were large land crabs everywhere, so they built huts from screw pines with roofs of leaves, and lived on coconuts, *midili* nuts, birds, turtles and reef fish.

But they longed for bananas and sweet potatoes from home, and they missed their children and families. So, they scratched their names and the word '*Hoḷḷavai*' into strips of palm leaves and at night went to where the frigatebirds were nesting. It stank of guano, but they held their noses and tied the messages to the birds' feet while they slept. A week later, the frigatebirds migrated north in a great black cloud and landed in the Maldives. A boy in Fuvahmulah caught one, showed the message to his parents, and three boats were sent to rescue the lost Maldivians.

One hundred years later, a French ship loaded with slaves from Madagascar and Mozambique landed on the uninhabited Chagos Islands, where they were forced to work in coconut plantations. They were followed a few years later by the British, who established a trading post for slave ships sailing from Malaysia to the Seychelles via Mauritius, long after slavery was abolished. Hidden from the eyes of the world, the slaves developed an African French creole language and called themselves *Ilois* (Islanders). They named Chagos the 'Isles of Shame', and the colonialists the 'British Vampire'.

In 1965 the British Government bought the Chagos Islands shortly before they granted independence to Mauritius, and then leased the largest island in the archipelago, Diego Garcia, to the US military to build an airbase. The descendants of the *Ilois* were forced to leave their homes and were dumped on the docks in Mauritius without the compensation they had been promised.

They were regarded as outcasts, and many migrated to Crawley, near London, where their cause has been supported by the poet Benjamin Zephaniah. In 2021, the UN court ruled that Britain had no sovereignty over the Chagos Islands, following the International Court of Justice ordering the British Government to hand them back to Mauritius in 2019. The *Ilois* are still waiting.

I was introduced to this story by my friend Josian, storyteller, actor and nurse from Mauritius, who was invited by the British Government to work in the NHS in Wales. At the end of his seven-year contract, Josian was informed his services were no longer required and he would be deported. He found himself caught in the government's 'hostile environment', but with the help of a civil rights lawyer he won a legal case and was granted British citizenship. He celebrated by strolling along the promenade in Aberystwyth dressed in a pin-stripe suit and a monocle, greeting passers-by with a cheery 'chin-chin'. Around the same time, Aberystwyth University opened a campus in Port Louis, Mauritius, only to close two years later having lost £1 million amidst criticism of contemporary colonialism.

'*Zistoire ième av tourtie dans bord bassin léroi*' is a popular tale in Mauritius, a slave narrative and satire on colonial authority from an 1888 collection of Creole folktales by Charles Baissac, a descendant of French colonisers and, ironically, a supporter of slavery. It features the African trickster Hare, and his old running mate, Tortoise.

The King of Mauritius liked a mug of hot chocolate after his daily swim. One morning, he walked down to the pond on his plantation, only to find the water was filthy, as if someone had dumped sewage in it. He ordered his servant to clean it up, but next day, the water was even muddier. The king said, 'I want my hot chocolate in a mug, not in my bath. Clean it properly! Or else!'

Rooster, Goose and Dog were watching.

Rooster said, 'It's the fairies, Mr Servant.'

Goose added, 'The fairies don't like rich folks.'

Dog barked, 'They turned a boy from Crève Cœur into a mountain.'

So, the servant sieved all the mud out of the pond, but by the third day, it looked like a cesspit. The king said, 'I'll catch a virus if I swim in that. I want a nice clean bath. I'm beginning to smell. If it's like that in the morning, I'll cut off your head.'

Rooster said, 'Careful, Mr Servant.'

Goose added, 'The king likes cutting off heads.'

Dog barked, 'I prefer my head where it is, on my shoulders.'

That night the servant hid by the pond and waited to see if he could catch the offender. He heard footsteps and singing, tip-tapping and rip-rapping along the road, and there, silhouetted in the moon, was old trickster, Leuk, the Hare.

Hare held out a calabash, 'Hey Mr Servant, have some honey.'

The servant didn't trust Hare, but he loved honey, so he ate a big spoonful and said, 'That's fine honey, Mr Hare.'

'It's from my parents in Trois Ilots! And I've added something a little special.'

'I'm glad you haven't taken it from the king's beehives,' said the servant.

'Oh no, Mr Servant, the king would cut my head off. Here, have some more.'

The servant ate the lot, stretched, yawned and fell fast asleep.

Hare rubbed his paws together, took the herbal sleeping potion out of his pocket, kissed it, laid his towel on the bank, put on his swimming goggles, dived into the pond, splashed about and stirred up the mud, until it looked like the king's mug of hot chocolate. Then Hare climbed out, dried himself, tip-tapped down the road and climbed back into the moon.

In the morning, the servant woke to find a mud bath, and he vanished before the king had a chance to decapitate him.

Next day, the king advertised for a new servant at eight piastres a month, money that could only be spent in his own shop. Nobody applied for the job.

Rooster said, 'I don't like the pay.'

Goose added, 'I'm not gonna be anyone's servant.'

Dog barked, 'I want to keep my head.

So, each night Hare stirred up the mud, and each day the king smelled worse and worse.

Then, someone applied for the job.

'You're a tortoise?' said the king.

'It's the shell. It's a giveaway, isn't it? Please, no jokes about meat pies,' said Tortoise.

'You can't look after a pond!'

'Yes I can, my mother was a terrapin. And you smell like you need a bath!'

'That's because my pond water is dirty. Clean it up or I'll cut off your head!'

'You'll have to find it first,' said Tortoise, and she tucked it into her shell.

Tortoise talked to Rooster, Goose and Dog, and they cleaned up the pond and hatched a plan. They painted Tortoise's shell with tar, and at sunset she sat by the roadside next to the pond, tucked in her head and waited.

Hare jumped off the moon, and as he tip-tapped and rip-rapped down the road, he saw a black sticky thing by the pond. 'Hey! What a nice King. He's put this rock by the water so I can sit and dry myself after my swim.'

Hare sat on the rock. It moved. 'Hey! My bench wobbles! You just can't get servants in Mauritius anymore!' Hare wedged a piece of wood under the rock, and his arm stuck to the tar. He tried to pull himself free and his other arm stuck, too.

Tortoise popped her head out of her shell. 'Leuk, old friend! How you doin'? I haven't seen you since I beat you in that race.'

'Tortoise, mon ami! You only won 'cos I had a nap. Like some honey?'

'No thank you. You look like you're stuck to a rock?'

'I'm fine,' and Hare tried to pull himself off with his left leg. Bam! Then his right leg. Bam! Now he was really stuck. Two legs and two arms glued to a rock.

'Hold on tight, Mr Hare, we're goin' walkies,' said Tortoise.

Hare looked out of the page at Ms Storyteller.

'Hey, Storyteller Lady! Get me out of this. I'm stuck to Tortoise. And I'm Hare, the smartest animal around, my people need me.'

Ms Storyteller shook her head, 'You got yourself in this mess, Mr Hare.'

Tortoise kept on walking and Hare kept on talking.

'Listen, Tortoise, my legs and arms may be stuck, but I've a very hard head, and I'll squash you like a ripe pawpaw and we'll be eating tortoise-meat pie!' Bam! Hare headbutted tortoise. And now his head was stuck.

Tortoise kept on walking with Hare glued to the top of her shell, down to the pond where Rooster, Dog, and Goose were waiting. 'Go tell the king we got him,' said Tortoise.

Dog ran off, and how the king laughed when he saw Hare stuck to Tortoise.

Rooster said, 'Jugged hare tonight, Mr King?'

Goose added, 'With a little red wine from Morrisons?'

Dog barked, 'And I'll keep my head on my shoulders where it feels nice!'

The king licked his lips.

Hare said, 'Tortoise, you're not gonna let this old plantation owner eat your friend Leuk? I'll give you all my honey if you let me go.'

Tortoise said, 'It's a deal. I love honey. Especially from Trois Ilots.'

So, Rooster, Goose and Dog pulled Hare free from Tortoise's shell and pushed the king in the pond. He splashed around, 'Get me out! I'm drowning in mud!'

'Serves you right, King,' said Tortoise, 'You came over here and dumped your sewage in our water, and you threaten to cut off our heads if we complain. You've made this mess for yourself, so have a swim in your muddy pond, while we feast on Hare's honey and your wine.'

And that's how independence came to Mauritius.

In 2014, it was revealed that for three decades, the American Navy had dumped hundreds of tonnes of sewage and wastewater into a protected lagoon on Diego Garcia, the largest of the Chagos Islands, another act of environmental vandalism perpetrated on the Isles of Shame by friends of the British Vampire.

21

Weretiger

KHASI

Long ago, when people and beasts and stones and trees spoke as one, a man in the East Khasi hills of Meghalaya in north-east India was given a written message from God containing religious teachings, philosophies and ritual instructions. He lost it on his journey home, but he had memorised every word, and so began the Khasi tradition of education and entertainment through oral storytelling, using *khana pateng* (legends), *purinam* (fairy tales), *puriskam* (fables) and *khana pharshi* (parables), which was far easier than writing stuff down.

Not quite so long ago, on 22 June 1842, a time when some people saw themselves as superior to lowly animals, another man, a miller and wheelwright from Llangynyw in Wales arrived in the clouds of Sohra, in Meghalaya, along with his pregnant wife, Anne. He was a Presbyterian missionary, Thomas Jones, who, in his short life, translated the Bible into Khasi, helped create a written alphabet for the language and taught basic carpentry, stonemasonry, blacksmith-ing, agricultural innovations and brewing rice beer, *kiadsaw*, much to the displeasure of the British authorities who he had condemned for their behaviour towards the Khasi.

When Anne died in childbirth in 1846, Thomas was dismissed from the mission for marrying a 15-year-old British girl, although the matrilineal Khasi did not forget him. A weathered folksy statue stands by the roadside in Sohra showing a handsome young man in a white coat, blue trousers rolled up to the knee, a saw in one hand and book in the other, in stark contrast to the usual monumental stone erections to British imperialists. And in Meghalaya, 22 June is celebrated annually as Thomas Jones Day.

Jones was no stereotypical imperialist, and as a Welshman, he would not have described himself as such, yet there is an inevitable sense of 'white saviour' about his story. Although many Khasi turned to Christianity, others balanced the new religion with the old ways. They

worked the land, grew crops, carved wood and smelted iron long before the missionaries arrived, and believed that while people had souls, so did rocks, plants and animals. When their oral stories were collected by ethnographers in books of myths and legends, the old meanings were lost, leaving only fantastical narratives, texts without context.

The tale of 'Dirty Pig' is generic in Meghalaya, so I've woven in some stories based on the contemporary research of Desmond Karmawphlang in Ri Bhoi, north of Sohra, through his interviews with U Diseng Marin of Pahamshken, U Joid Makri of Pahambir, and U Sarot Maji, late of Mawphrew. They are *Khla Phuli*, Tigermen, whose souls, *karngiew*, or shadows, *syrngiew*, enter wild creatures, often through dreams. The worlds of people and animals are intricately entwined, not separated by theologies and philosophies. Should an animal with a human soul be killed, the human dies too.

Tiger was King of the monsoon-soaked Cherrapunji Forest at Sohra. Leopard, Elephant and Rhinoceros respected him, Water Buffalo, Swamp Deer and Pig-tailed Macaque feared him, while Fish Eagle, Hornbill and Stork watched him warily from high branches.

Tiger padded across the tangled tree-root bridges, lashed his tail to shake the rainwater from his fur, and smiled through shining teeth at everyone he met, for he only killed when his belly grumbled. His brothers and sisters had been hunted for trophies, their skins made into rugs, bones ground down for medicine, and yet he was a hunter himself, no different to men. They all ate the same food.

One evening Tiger ate a whole water buffalo and wandered down to the waterhole for a drink. Washing herself in the shallows was a young wild pig and when she saw Tiger, she held her breath, froze and closed her eyes, hoping he wouldn't see her if she couldn't see him.

Tiger licked his lips, 'I have room in my belly for a little pork rice before bedtime.' He prowled along the line of banyan trees and was just about to leap when his body stiffened. 'No, not now!' and he slipped back into the forest as the moon rose and lay down as the shadow of the *Khla Phuli* entered his mind and body.

His paws grew a fifth claw, the only outward sign of possession. He must go to the village and protect the people and their land and chase away the *dkhars*. His after-dinner snack would have to wait. He was now *Khla Phuli*, Weretiger.

At the waterhole, Little Pig looked up and realised Tiger had vanished without eating her. A thought struck her, 'Tiger is afraid of me.' She ran around shouting, 'I've beaten Tiger in battle. He's too old. I will be King now. No, I will be Queen!' She called into the forest. 'Tiger, bow before me.'

Tiger peered over Little Pig's shoulder and whispered, 'I'm busy right now, meet me here tomorrow, and we'll see who is King.'

Little Pig twirled her tail at him and bounced off singing, 'I'm Queen now!' over and over again.

The other animals watched with eyes as big as waterholes. Had Little Pig defeated Tiger? If so, how?

Elephant said, 'Tiger has weapons of fangs, claws and whiskers. He eats people and pigs alike.'

Rhinoceros added, 'Tiger probably wasn't hungry. He'll eat you for breakfast tomorrow.'

Water Buffalo continued, 'You're so little, you're only a snack to Tiger.'

Stork agreed, 'If Tiger doesn't boil you up, Durokma will.'

Leopard grinned, 'The people sing ballads about Durokma. She lives in a cave in the Garos Hills and is worshipped as Matchama, Tiger Mother. She'll make you into *Dohkileh*, pig brain curry. If she can find your brain.'

And all the animals laughed at Little Pig.

She ran to Grandfather Pig and told him how she had defeated Tiger and was now Queen. Grandfather bowed his head and thought for a moment. He spoke:

'The Tiger God, Lathari, cares for the Makdoh people and watches over them in the fields and markets unseen. When anyone dies, Lathari mourns with them by the pyre.

'Tiger helped Rynjang of the Khonglah escape from the *Kyrdep Tarang* by hiding her inside the trunk of the *dymbui* tree. The Khonglahs eat neither tigers nor people, nor cut down the dymbui tree.

'A Kunongrim woman was trapped on a cliff ledge until Tiger lowered his tail down for her to climb like a rope. She never ate tiger meat again, and named herself Laitmiet, "freed at night".

'Tigers help people. There is a man in the village whose soul leaves him at night-time and enters Tiger's body. He is no shapeshifter, nor does he practice metamorphosis or magical arts. His spirit-shadow controls Tiger through the strength of his ancestors and the forest. People, animals and trees are One.'

Little Pig considered this seriously, 'Does that mean Tiger will help me?'

'No', said Grandfather, 'He's going to eat you.'

Little Pig turned white.

Grandfather continued, 'And if Tiger doesn't eat you, the people will. They love roast pork.'

'No, I want to grow old and wise like you and write a book. I can't do that if they eat my brains.'

Grandfather thought, 'Well, roll yourself in mud till you are dirty, and wait for Tiger.'

'Will that work?'

'No idea. Let's find out.'

Little Pig ran to the waterhole and rolled around in the mud, and after she stopped giggling, she rolled again, until she was one big mound of muddy pig.

Tiger lay curled up asleep on the roof of the *Khla Phuli*'s house in the village. He had spent the night chasing coal-diggers, lime-dusters and charcoal-burners from the forest. As the sun rose, the shadow-soul was leaving his body and returning to the vivid dreams of the man sleeping below. The man's father had inhabited Tiger many years before, and so would his son and daughter in years to come. As Tiger woke, he remembered he had promised himself pork rice for breakfast. He leapt from the roof, leaving pieces of fur and a few *betel* leaves behind.

In the house, the man was dreaming. The televisions and phones that had supplanted the hearth as the centre of storytelling were reporting on breakfast news about tribal protests against *dhkars* (non-tribals), who were moving into Shillong, drowning out the traffic jams and loud music of India's rock capital. There was anger and violence in those sounds.

The man shook his head, for he knew people and beasts and stones and trees all have the same souls. They should listen to the forest. He awoke, checked his mobile for messages, and for some reason, had a craving for *Dohneiiong*, pork curry.

When Tiger arrived at the waterhole, he found a muddy piggy mound in front of him. It spoke, 'I'm Queen, and I'm going to fight you, Tiger.'

This was so far beneath Tiger's dignity. He roared half-heartedly and walked away in search of less dirty food.

And that's why all pigs wallow in mud, not because they are unclean, but it saves them from being eaten by Weretiger.

22

Yakshi

Beyond the seven forests and seven mountains, Yakshi was fast asleep in the top of a palm tree by the side of the road from Thiruvananthapuram in Kerala to Padmanabhapuram on the way to Tamil Nadu, when she smelled him. She peered across the endless rice fields and there he was. A Namboodiri, a Brahmin, clutching a book of prayer, muttering in Sanskrit.

Night was falling. She scratched her hollow back, fastened the buttons on her blouse, brushed and pinned her hair, packed some betel leaves, areca nuts and spices in her bag, placed a sprig of jasmine in her bosom, put on her shoes, which was tricky because her feet pointed backwards, and rubbed her empty belly.

As she climbed down the trunk, she hummed the lullaby '*Omanathinkal Kidavo*' and thought of her sisters in the north, those sweet nature-spirits connected with water, fertility, trees, treasure, wilderness and the wellbeing of the forest, who served Kubera, the god of wealth and prosperity in Hindu, Buddhist and Jain mythology, whereas she was raised to be as ravishing as the girls in the Malayalam films and novels of Malayattoor Ramakrishnan. She was beautiful on the outside, nasty on the inside. She drained men's blood.

As the Namboodiri approached the tree, he quickened his step, for he knew there were soulless spirits in the rice fields, and it would be wise to be home before dark. The moon was already silver in the sky, the last bees of the day were gathering pollen from the flowers to make honey, a smell of jasmine was in his nose and it reminded him of the woman he was to marry.

He was the youngest in his family and was betrothed to a local girl, for custom forbade him to marry another Namboodiri, a right reserved for his elder brother. As his mind slipped from thoughts of the *Vedas*, he saw a voluptuous woman standing at the roadside beneath a palm tree. Or was it a *pala*, a devil tree?

'Oh, sir,' said Yakshi, leaning against the trunk, still trying to fasten the top button on her blouse, 'Night is coming, and I am afraid. May I walk with you?'

'Of course, my daughter,' he replied. He was alone with the scent of jasmine and a beautiful young woman.

She walked a step behind him, humming her lullaby.

'Do you devote yourself to our higher traditions, my child?'

'Of course, sir, I listen to the stories of my people who grow rice here.'

The Namboodiri looked sternly, 'Go to the temple and raise your eyes higher.' He walked faster, while Yakshi hurried to keep up. She watched as his loincloth flapped and his forelock bobbed in the gentle breeze. This could be fun, she thought.

'Do you know the story of Sreedevi?' he asked.

'Yes, she was a kind, caring and misunderstood woman like Purushadevi.'

'She was a prostitute and a vampire who preyed on an innocent young man, Raman, and tried to turn him away from the temple, but he was a brave man and he strangled her when they lay in bed one night, but she returned to drink the blood of noble men and gave birth to many more bad women.'

'Oh, surely there are no bad women here?' replied Yakshi, as the top button of her blouse popped open again. 'My mother taught me to sleep with my underwear beneath my nightgown, in case a Gandharva came down from heaven and seduced me with his unearthly music.'

'The Gandharvi are noble poets,' said Namboodiri, 'You should be honoured.'

Yakshi held up her skirt, 'Look, sir, I still have my underwear on.'

Namboodiri averted his gaze and strode on, with Yakshi making light conversation a few footsteps behind. 'Sir, when we reach the town, we will stop at my father's house and I will make a meal for your kindness. I have betel leaves, areca nuts and spices that I will fry in a pan. Perhaps you have a lime I can add?' Yakshi smiled and wiped her mouth, smearing the swiftly applied rouge across her cheek.

He may have been a brahmin, but the Namboodiri had enough experience of the world to know he couldn't refuse this offer, for he was aware of the symbolism of lime and betel leaves. But doubt gnawed at him. 'Do you know of Kadamattathu Kathanar?

'Will it be a love story?'

'In the days when this road to Padmanabhapuram was a narrow path through a jungle, people were afraid to walk after night fall, because a Yakshi lived in a *Pala* tree by the path. She enticed young men, and if they touched her, she turned into a vampire and drank their blood and ate their flesh.'

'So, not a love story?' said Yakshi.

'The noble priest Kadamattathu Kathanar decided to rid Kerala of this creature. He dressed as a traveller and walked till darkness fell, when the Yakshi appeared and even he was enchanted. She asked for a little lime and betel leaves, he offered it to her on the end of an iron nail to avoid touching her, knowing that iron would protect him. But she began to seduce him, so he drove the nail into her head. She fainted in his arms and became his slave.'

'Did she walk a few steps behind him?' asked Yakshi.

'Kathanar took her to Kayamkulam and gave her to his aunt, who cleaned her and combed her hair. Aunt found the nail in Yakshi's head and removed it. The girl vanished. When aunt told Kathanar what had happened, he followed Yakshi to Mannar, and found her crossing the River Pamba in a boat. Kathanar floated over the river on a big banana leaf, and confronted her. Overcome by his presence, she fell at his feet and promised never to hurt anyone again. The noble Kathanar took pity on her and gave her a temple, Panayannarkavu. She still appears to travellers on moonlit nights, but she has hurt no one since.'

'So, she is a good vampire now she has a soul,' said Yakshi, 'Have you seen the statue at Malampuzha? By Kanayi Kunhiraman? She's thirty feet high with enormous breasts and she sits like this.' Yakshi sat down in the road and spread her legs wide.

Namboodiri wondered whether this young woman even had a soul.

Yakshi stood up as demurely as she could and pointed to a *tharavad*, a rambling ancestral house by the roadside, not quite as grand as Padmanabhapuram Palace. 'Look, there's my father's house,'

'Ah, a nobleman's home,' said Namboodiri, who was reassured he had nothing to fear, for this girl, though vulgar, was daughter of an esteemed man.

Yakshi opened the door, Namboodiri walked inside and was surprised to find no furniture, not even a mattress on the floor. He was about to think that something was not quite right, when the door closed, and he turned round. The girl was smiling now, large white teeth shining between her bright red lips, and was that lipstick or blood around her mouth? She wiped it away and it blushed into the smudged rouge on her cheek. She sang '*Omanathinkal Kidavo*':

Is this sweet baby
The bright crescent moon, or the delicious lotus-flower?
The honey in a flower, or the silver of the full moon?

'Oh, this is too easy,' thought Yakshi. 'I don't even have to be a monster. I can play with him, spend a night of pleasure, then release him, for that would be the morally correct thing to do, wouldn't it? Or shall I do what my Kerala girlfriends are meant to do and tear him into little pieces. Though that would be wrong. Very wrong!'

Yakshi remembered a storyteller explaining that all tales must take people to a dark otherworld, but always return to kindness. She saw the terror in the Namboodiri's eyes, so she smiled, stroked his hair tuft and kissed him. 'Do you know of Purushadevi, daughter of the Queen of Pennarasunadu, a kingdom ruled by women?' asked Yakshi, 'When she became pregnant, a neighbouring king declared war on Pennarasunadu. With the battle almost lost, Purushadevi cut open her belly and threw her unborn child at the king, saying he had stolen it. He was so shamed, he killed himself in front of her.'

In the morning, amidst the birdsong, the lullaby '*Omanathinkal Kidavo*' floated round the palm tree on the road from Thiruvananthapuram to Padmanabhapuram. Namboodiri lay beneath, betel leaves between his stained teeth, smelling of lime, his hair tuft bitten off, completely drained of blood.

ഓമനത്തിങ്കള്‍ക്കിടാവോ- നല്ല കോമളത്താമരപ്പൂവോ
പൂവില്‍ നിറഞ്ഞ മധുവോ- പരിപൂര്‍ണേന്ദു
തന്റെ നിലാവോ
പുത്തന്‍ പവിഴക്കൊടിയോ- ചെറു
തത്തകള്‍ കൊഞ്ചും മൊഴിയോ

23

The Fox and the Ghost

中国, *ZHŌNGGUÓ*, CHINA

During the reign of the Kangxi Emperor in the late seventeenth century, a fire broke out at a shop that sold melon seeds. In the embers, lying side by side, were found the charred bodies of a man and his lover, a fox. This was the *huli jing*, 狐狸精, a fox spirit associated with the sex industry, a hidden male dreamworld as mythical as fairyland. Historian Guo Pu wrote that if a fox lived till it was 50, it transformed into a woman, and when 100, it seduced men during a night of animal passion in a brothel with a centenarian.

This story was written by Pu Song-ling, 蒲松齡, in his collection, *Strange Tales From a Chinese Studio*, originally titled *Tales of Ghosts and Foxes*. Pu was born in Zichuan, Shandong Province, in the shadow of Mount Tai in 1640, where he studied his whole life to be a scholar but failed all his exams. He worked for a pittance as a private tutor from his studio Liaozhai, in Zibo, where he offered passers-by tea and tobacco in exchange for supernatural tales. He never raised enough money to publish them in his lifetime, though he left behind the saying, 'Every Chinese intellectual has a Liaozhai in their hearts', a sentiment that continued through Mao Zedong's Cultural Revolution when Pu's characters appeared in books like, *Stories About Not Being Afraid of Ghosts* by Yang Xianyi in 1961, a thinly veiled attack on Western imperialism.

Pu's otherworldly figures of the fox and the ghost are both supernatural and human, and star in this story that Pu heard at an inn in Yizhou from his friend, Wang Tzŭ-chang, who had written a biography of a scholar, Mr Sang.

Sang Tzŭ-ming was orphaned young and lived alone in the Saffron Market near Yizhou, where he worked as a personal tutor and wrote weird tales and strange stories to expose the corruption and injustice that kept the world of the poor invisible to the wealthy. He preferred the company of books to people and ventured outside only to visit his neighbour for a meal twice a day.

Over a dinner conversation about the supernatural, Sang's neighbour asked what he would do if he ever met a fox or a ghost.

Sang laughed, 'I am a pragmatist. If they come as men, I have a sharp sword for them, and if as women, I have a warm bed waiting.'

The neighbour laughed at his friend's boasting and decided to play a trick. He paid a sing-song girl from the Western District to spend a night with Sang. That evening, she climbed over the fence and scratched at his door.

'Who's there?' cried Sang.

She giggled, 'I'm a ghost.'

'Go away! You can't scare me. I'm a scholar.'

At dinner next day, Sang spoke of his ghostly encounter, and his neighbour said, 'I thought you were keeping a bed warm for her?' Sang realised then it was a joke, but at least he wasn't being haunted by a ghost.

A few months later, Lien-hsiang climbed over Sang's fence, stood outside his door, peered into her looking glass, whitened her cheeks, reddened her lips, straightened her blue robe and went through her lines. 'I am from the floating dreamworld in the minds of men. I can write calligraphy, read haiku, perform tea ceremony, play backgammon and pluck the three-stringed *samisen*. I have worked since I was 14 and have outlived my sisters, who are usually dead at 20.'

She pouted into the looking glass. She was ready. Sang answered the door, and looked her up and down, 'Has my neighbour sent you?'

'I'm Lien-hsiang, Lotus Fragrance, come from your dreams. I'm very good with my hands. Look, aren't they small?'

'Yes, they're very nice. Are you sure my neighbour hasn't sent you?'

'You're lonely,' said Lien-hsiang, 'I'm here to pleasure you.'

She was from the Saffron Market brothels and she was elegant, so Sang invited her in, having first ensured his neighbour was watching. She stayed that night and many nights, yet always refused payment.

One day, Sang was waiting for Lien-hsiang when another girl climbed over the fence and stood at his door. 'Are you from my dreams?' he asked, 'I already have a friend from there.'

'My name is Li, and my parents are most respectable. I have heard of your reputation as a scholar. I wish to be your pupil.'

She didn't look like a sing-song girl. Her hair was down to the shoulders, her gown had long, flowing sleeves, and she glided gracefully across the floor. She offered her hand, which was like ice, 'It is cold outside, and I am delicate. Will you warm me?'

'Ah, she's a fox', thought Sang, 'she wants to get into my bed.'

During the night, Sang discovered Li was a virgin. In the morning, she gave him a tiny, embroidered slipper and told him if he warmed it in his hands, she would come, but not if his sing-song girl was there. As she left, he noticed she had lotus feet, bound from birth. How could women endure such pain, he thought, showing surprising sensitivity for a scholar.

Let me introduce myself. I am your storyteller, here to provide commentary and eliminate confusion. Mr Sang, a scholar, is being visited by two ladies. A sing-song girl who is really a fox, and a 'respectable' girl who Sang thinks is a fox, but isn't. Simple.

Next day, when Sang was alone, he held the slipper, and Li walked in. She visited Sang for ten nights, until he told her about Lien-hsiang.

'Is she as beautiful as the moon? Or me?' Li asked as she lay in his arms.

'She is a little warmer than you,' replied Sang.

Sang, like most scholars, is not renowned for social skills.

'Be careful, my love, Lien-hsiang is a fox. She will draw the breath from you,' and Li flounced out.

That evening, Lien-hsiang lay in Sang's bed, 'Someone has slept here?'

'How can you tell?' asked Sang.

'I can smell her. And look in the mirror. You're emaciated, drained of life.'

'My friend thinks you are a fox.'

'And what's the difference between a fox and a woman, Mr Scholar?'

'Well,' answered Sang, coming over all academic, 'foxes have the power to seduce people and draw the life from them, and therefore must be feared.'

'Honey, three nights making love with me and you'll live to be 100.'

I hope you're taking notes? Now you know how to live a long life.

Sang told Lien-hsiang all about Li.

'Be careful, baby, your little Li is no fox. She's a ghost. She will suck the breath from you. And it'll be no fun if you're dead.'

'You're just jealous because I love Li!'

Lien-hsiang hit Sang with a pillow, dressed, transformed into a fox and left.

So Lien-hsiang is a fox, but is Li a ghost?

Sang held the slipper, Li appeared and she wasn't happy.

'Why have you kept me away?'

'Lieng-hsiang tells me you are a ghost and are sucking the breath from me.'

'That nasty fox,' cried Li, 'She has infected you. Get rid of her, or I will not come again.'

'No. I love you,' called Sang, but Li flounced out again.

Don't worry, Li will return. For this is my cunning plot device to bring together the fox and ghost from their two weird and strange worlds.

Lying in bed that night, Lien-hsiang told Sang stories about life in the Saffron Market, how the girls were bought and sold by businessmen, how the lead in the white face paint ate their skin, and yet it was still preferable to a life of rural poverty. She asked Sang to help her expose the cruelty and corruption, so the girls could manage their own lives. 'They will listen to you, Mr Scholar.'

Sang was intrigued. He loved an injustice, but his love for Li distracted him. His silence spoke volumes. Lien-hsiang dressed and walked to the door, 'I'm going away for 100 days. Don't let Dead-girl suck you dry. I need you.' And she transformed into a fox and vanished.

Oh, Mr Sang! Who to believe, fox or ghost?

Li the ghost stayed with Sang every night for two months until he was so weak, he was bedridden. After 100 days, the screen opened and Lien-hsiang the fox appeared, 'Mr Scholar, you're still breathing?'

Sang confessed, 'You were right about Li. I'm dying. Please help me!'

'Only the ghost who's draining your life can cure you, and that's Ms Death!'

Sang held the slipper, Li walked in, and Lien-hsiang blocked the doorway to prevent her leaving, 'Who are you, lotus foot? Why do you want to kill Sang?'

'I am the daughter of Judge Li. I died young and was buried beneath the wall outside Sang's house, neither in this world or the other. Like the silkworm locked in its cocoon before it can spin its thread, my destiny is unfulfilled. I don't wish Sang dead. I love him.'

Ah, but constant love can drain a human!

'Ghost, your lovemaking is killing him!' said the fox.

'No, Fox, your scheming is killing him!' replied the ghost.

Lien-hsiang stared at Li, 'If Sang dies, I'll make sure you'll join him! Imagine what a chicken coop would look like after a visit from me.'

'If Sang dies, we would never be together. Ghosts can only be with the living. I would have to haunt you!'

Fox and ghost faced each other with ice in their eyes and blood red lips.

Sang interrupted, 'Excuse me, ladies, but when you've finished discussing who is the nastiest, remember I'm the one who's dying.' And he coughed.

You see, people don't need foxes or ghosts to hurt them. They are quite capable of damaging themselves, and everyone around them.

Lien-hsiang produced a bottle of pills from her bag. 'These will save Sang, but they must be given by the one who poisoned him. And that's you, honey.' She placed a pill on Li's tongue and told her to kiss Sang. Li flushed, but Lien-hsiang said, 'You've kissed him many times. One more will cure him.'

Li slipped her tongue into Sang's mouth and he swallowed the pill. His insides blazed, his bowels exploded and he was turned inside out until sunrise, when he lay back, exhausted.

Fox and ghost slept in Sang's bed together for three months till he recovered. Then Li vanished and never returned, and even Lien-hsiang pined for that strange icy creature who never removed her gown.

Li was not in her grave. She woke in the body of Yen-êrh, the 15-year-old daughter of wealthy Mr and Mrs Zhang. Lien-hsiang the fox returned in the body of Wei, a fish-cutter's daughter. And they will both continue to vanish and return, living through more weird tales and strange stories.

See them, the fox, the ghost and the scholar, walking arm-in-arm through the deserted fairy-tale amusement park in Beijing, another of China's lost worlds.

24

Yōkai

日本, *NIHON*, JAPAN

I met Pyonky Nishiziri, *kamishibai* illustrator and master of the art of Japanese visual storytelling, at Beyond the Border International Storytelling Festival a few years ago. We had no shared languages so communicated by showing drawings to each other. Pyonky pointed to a coffee cup ring on one of my sketches and laughed as he pulled out one of his *kamishibai* drawings, also stained with a coffee ring. In that moment, we understood our artwork was not precious, it could be thrown around, used as place mats or for emergency shopping lists, and art and visual storytelling were universal languages.

Kamishibai appeared in the Shitamachi section of Tokyo around 1930, when storytellers rode round on bicycles, set up their toy theatres in alleyways and streets, enticed audiences with free homemade sweets and told stories while they showed hundreds of illustrations, drawn in a style that evolved into manga and anime. Shigeru Mizuki was born in Osaka in 1922 and rented out his illustrations to *kamishibaiya*, drawn with his right hand after he lost his dominant left arm in an Allied air raid in Papua New Guinea, where he was serving as a soldier. His most popular characters were Yōkai, Japanese otherworldly spirits that appeared only in times of peace and became an expression of Mizuki's pacifism, which was strengthened by the horror of the American H-bombs that devastated Hiroshima and Nagasaki.

Yōkai were also called upon by Hayao Mayazaki, master storyteller and animator, who featured them in his iconic film *Princess Mononoke* as the little white forest spirits, the *kodama*, developed from his childhood memory of Yakushima Island.

The story below was told by Koizumi Setsu, daughter of a samurai from Matsue, to her husband, the writer and teacher Lafcadio Hearn, who published it in 1903 in his five-volume collection of *Japanese Fairy Tales*. Hearn was born in Greece, raised

in Ireland, lived in the radical underworld of Cincinnati and New
Orleans, before moving to Japan in 1890 when he was 40. He
changed his name to Koizumi Yakumo and wrote a popular illustrated book based on the fairy tale 'The Boy Who Drew Cats'.
Setsu and Hearn lived through Japan's culture change from feudal
to industrial during the final days of the samurai, when they called
on the Yōkai.

Once there was a lazy girl whose parents were so rich, she had
servants to do everything for her. They dressed and undressed her,
brushed and arranged her hair, and made her look so pretty that
no one noticed how lazy she was. Her grandmother gave her the
beautiful family dolls she had played with as a child, but Lazy-girl
left them lying all over the floor for the servants to tidy up. Worst of
all, after she ate her candy and cleaned her teeth, she hid the dirty
toothpicks in the weave of the reed mats, which annoyed the servants who had to clean the floor so the family could sit on it to eat
their dinner.

When she grew up, Lazy-girl's parents married her to a poor
samurai who had only one servant, and so she became an *okuga-
tasama*, a woman who looked after her own household. She had to
dress herself, tidy her clothes and brush her own hair, which was
difficult, but she managed, although cooking, keeping the accounts
and caring for her in-laws were quite beyond her.

Her husband was frequently away on business. He was a follower
of Saigō Takamori and the Satsuma Rebellion at the time of the
Meigi Restoration when the samurai were discussing whether to
accept westernisation or prepare for battle with the modernisers to
maintain their traditional way of life.

Lazy-girl enjoyed her husband's absence. She left her hair in a
mess, scattered her clothes all over the floor and didn't care whether
anyone picked them up. She copied drawings of fox-girls from her
books of fairy tales onto handmade paper, though she frequently
spilled her ink on the reed mats and stained her fingers with red
ochre. She taught herself how to handle a *naginata*, the weapon of

choice of women warriors, *onna-bugeisha*, so she could fight along-side her husband when the wars came – anything to avoid tidying up her toothpicks.

One night, at the Hour of the Ox, two o'clock, she was asleep in bed when she was awoken by strange noises. She lit a paper lantern and saw, dancing around on her pillow, hundreds of tiny men, dressed as samurai, each carrying a sword, with hair tied in man-buns. They laughed and sang as they danced:

> *Chin-chin Kobakama,*
> *Yomo fuké soro,*
> *Oshizumare, Hime-gimi!*
> *Ya ton ton!*

'Stop that, it's rude!' and she tried to swat them away.

They climbed on her, stuck their tongues out, pulled faces and tied her hair in knots. She chased them round the room, but they were too quick and there were so many of them, and they pricked her feet with their swords, singing:

> *Chin-chin Kobakama,*
> *Yomo fuké soro,*
> *Oshizumare, Hime-gimi!*
> *Ya ton ton!*

'Not listening!' and she leapt back into bed, pulled the pillow over her head and lay there till morning, when they vanished.

Lazy-girl thought these little men might be *yanari*, the Yōkai who made the house creak, or the *zashiki-warashi*, the Yōkai who lurked in the spare room. If only she was a *kitsune*, like the fox-girl, who was a sex worker and earned a fortune for her brothelkeeper even though he paid her a pittance.

So, one day, she turned into a fox and ran away to live with the poor woodcutter she loved. That night they hatched a plan. The woodcutter went to the brothel and paid for the services of the popular fox-girl. When the brothelkeeper couldn't find her, he had to pay double the money in compensation for services not rendered.

So, the woodcutter was a little richer and the brothelkeeper a little poorer, all thanks to the clever *kitsune*.

That night, at the Hour of the Ox, the Chin-chin Kobakama returned, and there were even more of them, and they sang:

Chin-chin Kobakama,
Yomo fuké soro.
Oshizumare …

'Stop!' shouted Lazy-girl as she pulled on her nose and tugged her ears, 'I'm a *kitsune* and I order you to go away, or I'll eat you!' The Chin-chin Kobakama laughed till their bellies ached and they tormented her all night long, while she lay with her head under the pillow.

That night she dreamed she met a woman wearing a face mask, a *kuchisake-onna*, who asked, '*Watashi, kirei*? (Am I pretty?)'

Lazy-girl replied, 'You're wearing a mask. How would I know?'

The woman removed her mask to reveal a mouth slit from ear to ear. '*Kore demo*? (How about now)?'

Lazy-girl knew this was a Yōkai from the future, and if she said the wrong words her own mouth would be slit in a never-ending smile. She fumbled in her pocket for some sugar candy, and said, 'Have some *bekko ame*.'

The woman ate the candy and opened her enormous mouth to eat Lazy-girl, who woke from her dream fearing of a world without samurai.

That evening, at the Hour of the Ox, the Chin-chin Kobakama climbed up through the gaps in the mats on the floor, and danced and sang:

Chin-chin Kobakama,
Yomo fuké …

'Stop!' said Lazy-girl, and she laughed, with her mouth almost as wide as the masked woman, leapt out of bed and drew her *naginata*. The Chin-chin Kobakama stopped in their tracks and stared at this giant warrior. Lazy-girl pulled a handful of candy out of her pocket and threw it on the floor, and said, 'If you don't go away, I will smear this whole mat with sticky candy, and you will be glued to it forever.'

With the candy exploding down on them like hard rain, the Chin-chin Kobakama scattered across the floor, turned into toothpicks, and disappeared into the sticky gaps between the reed mats, where they lived.

And there they are, watching for more toothpicks to drop onto their reed mat, but this was 1877, and Lazy-girl and her husband had left home to join the Battle of Mount Shiroyama, the final days of the Satsuma Rebellion, as Japan's feudal system ended with the defeat of the samurai.

25

Patupaiarehe

Around 1,000 years ago, Kupe and Kuramārōtini left their fishing grounds in Hawaiki and chased a giant octopus down the west coast of North Island to the Cook Strait. They entered Wellington Harbour and landed on Motukairangi Island, long before an earthquake raised the seabed in the fifteenth century and joined it to the mainland.

Kuramārōtini christened this new land Aotearoa, 'the long white cloud', and she named two nearby islands after her daughters, Matiu and Mākaro, while Kupe named a sharp pinnacle rock 'Te Ure o Kupe' after his penis, which he injured trying to land his *waka* canoe. In Māori oral myths, they were the first Polynesians in New Zealand.

The area is now the wealthy Wellington suburb of Miramar, where a carved wooden *pouwhenua* stands at the harbour entrance in honour of Kupe and Kuramārōtini, in contrast to the statue of Gandalf the Wizard, who guards the nearby art deco Roxy cinema near Peter Jackson's film studios where *Lord of the Rings* was made. Along the coast is Red Rocks, where Makaro's menstrual blood coloured the sea, and where in 2018 I watched as a Māori boy caught a small octopus that his family barbecued on the beach, just as Kupe and Kuramārōtini had centuries earlier, though without heavy metal booming from the speakers in their van.

Māori oral tales tell of another people who lived deep in the forests and bush of Aotearoa and high on the mountains of Taranaki, Pukemoremore and Pirongia. The Patupaiarehe were fair skinned, yellow or red haired, spoke a language understood by Māori and only ventured out at night or on misty days when they played flutes and sang haunting songs. They taught Māori how to weave fishing nets from flax and make tightly woven cloth until they were renowned as the finest weavers.

This tale was told by Te Matahaere, former guerrilla soldier and bush scout from Weriweri, by Rotorua Lake, to the historian and journalist

James Cowan, who was brought up speaking Te Aro Māori on a farm in Kihikihi, and who in 1925, wrote *Fairy Folk Tales of the Māori*.

Īhenga lived with his wife by Lake Rotorua and one day while exploring the nearby mountain, his throat became dry through breathing the fern pollen. A young woman offered him water from a calabash she had carried from the well by the lake and invited him to meet her Patupaiarehe family who lived in the *pā* on the mountaintop. The Patupaiarehe greeted him in peace, and he noticed that while some resembled Māori, others had the blue eyes and red hair of Pākehā, and they wore red-dyed clothes woven from flax. They offered him inanga fish from Lake Rotorua, which they ate raw for they disliked the nasty smell of Māori cooking.

They touched and stroked Īhenga, who thought they were going to marry him to the girl or eat him alive, and he feared he would never see his family again, so he made his excuses and fled down the mountain. As the Patupaiarehe chased him, he suddenly remembered he had a bottle of evil-smelling *kokowai*, shark oil mixed with red ochre, which he used to paint his skin. He scattered the oil as he ran, and the Patupaiarehe stopped, held their noses and retreated. When Īhenga reached home, he cooked the nastiest-smelling food and spread it round the house to keep the hidden people away. And he named the mountain Ngongotahā (a drink from the calabash).

I first encountered the Patupaiarehe through the *Pākehā* storyteller and writer Moira Wairama, who I visited with my son at her local *marae* in Stokes Valley at Christmas 2019 to tell tales of the Welsh Tylwyth teg. We were joined by Moira's partner, storyteller and actor Tony Hopkins, whose roots are in his own Black Cherokee tradition of the little people, the Yunwi tsunsdi. So, there we were, three storytellers from three continents with tales of three tribes of little people fermenting in our minds. Another story was about to begin.

We arrived at the *marae* to be told a funeral was taking place in the wharenui, the communal house next door. Māori *tangi* take around three days to allow time to remember the ancestors and prepare for the transition between worlds in a culture where life expectancy is considerably lower than amongst the *Pākehā*. Death is not hidden away behind a crematorium curtain or a cardboard eco-coffin as it is back home but celebrated as part of life.

We offered to cancel our storytelling out of sympathy, but the bereaved family gave us permission to go ahead if we paid our respects to their loved one. So, we left our shoes on the wooden porch where children were noisily playing cricket, and entered the *wharenui*, a great hall with carved wooden walls painted with characters from the myths of the tribal ancestors.

The family lay on cushions around the open casket and were introduced to us through spontaneous singing and oral storytelling in *Te Reo*, the Māori language, while we sat on a row of chairs and Moira translated quietly in our ears. Her nephew Simon replied on behalf of the strangers, voices ebbed and flowed like the tide, and time was no longer linear. After a while, half an hour, maybe an hour, we gathered round the casket, rubbed noses, kissed cheeks and the mood transformed from formality into one of warmth and party.

We left a *koha*, a monetary offering, and returned to the meeting room next door, where an audience of Māori and *Pākehā* were waiting to meet the Tylwyth teg and the Patupaiarehe. The stories I planned to tell felt insensitive to the moment, so I asked Simon about the lady in the casket, and he explained he knew little about her, other than she lived alone in the hills above Upper Hutt. He was extemporising, finding connections to join communities. So, I told the tale of 'Siani Pob Man', an old lady who lived on the beach at Cei Bach, where she fought against authority, cared for the local children and looked after her chickens, a story I hoped would be company on the lady's journey from casket to otherworld. This whole day had emerged from the world of shadows.

Te Kanawa, a chief of Waikato, was hunting kiwi on Mount Pukemoremore when darkness fell. He lit a fire and slept beneath the roots of a *rimu* tree but was woken by voices and sounds of children playing. Te Kanawa knew this was the Patupaiarehe, and his first thought was to run because they were mischief, but he was surrounded on a lonely mountain in the midst of dense bush.

The Patupaiarehe approached Te Kanawa, singing and chanting, and he was unsure whether they were greeting him or about to eat him. He blew on the fire till it blazed brightly and the Patupaiarehe retreated, but when it burnt low, they returned. Te Kanawa jabbed a stick into the ground and decorated it with his necklace with a carved greenstone figure, his matching greenstone earrings and a shark-tooth ring, which he offered as gifts. He stepped back.

The Patupaiarehe stopped singing and chanting, carefully stretched out their hands towards the stick, took hold of the shadows of the ornaments cast by the fire and ran into the bush, leaving behind the necklace, earrings and shark tooth. Patupaiarehe lived, peacefully, hidden in the shadows.

◦◦

'The white man in his covetousness ordered me to move on instead of removing himself from my presence. I resisted; I resist to this day … Ask that mountain, Taranaki saw it all!'

These words were spoken in 1903 by Te Whiti o Rongomai, and they tell of another hidden peaceful people. In 1866, Te Whiti and Tohu Kākahi founded Parihaka, a pacifist settlement at the foot of Mount Taranaki on land stolen from them during the New Zealand Wars. It was built on the ideals of the peaceful Moriori people of Rēkohu, whose land Taranaki Māori had migrated to fifty years earlier when forced from their own home. Soon, 2,000 Māori from different tribes came to Parihaka to plough the land, harvest the sea, become self-sufficient in food, have their own police force and bank, and live in equality, shrouded from colonial eyes.

In May 1879, the government decided to reclaim Mount Taranaki for settlers, fenced off land around Parihaka and built roads across the Waimate Plains. Te Whiti and Tohu rebelled, not with guns but with ploughs. They moved the fences across the roads to block government traffic, while the Māori ploughmen continued their agrarian revolution. The authorities moved in, 216 Māori were arrested and sent to South Island gaols.

'*Totoia*' means a person dragged around a paddock by horses; '*Te Iwi Herehere*', imprisoned people; '*Ngarukeruke*', a discarded body.

Taranaki Māori told tales of a giant eagle, Pouakai, who terrorised the land, eating flightless moa and killing children, until a visiting chief, Te Hauotawera, saw fear in the people and resolved to help. One dark night, he laid large manuka leaves and silver fern fronds over a deep pool, and in the morning, he stood in the middle of the pool until Pouakai appeared. As its talons were about to tear into him, Te Hauotawera leapt to one side and Pouakai crashed into the reflection of the moon in the pool, where it drowned.

By 1881, around 1,500 troops from the Constabulary Field Force surrounded Parihaka, set up a cannon on a nearby hill, stocked up on ammunition and rations, and waited. The *Taranaki Herald* exhorted them to 'make short work of the native difficulty by simply rubbing out the natives'.

On 5 November, the Taranaki Māori sat quietly in the Parihaka *marae* as the troops marched in. They had no wish to fight this threatening monster, so the children wore white albatross feathers, *raukura*, in their hair to symbolise peace, and greeted the soldiers with songs, while the women offered fresh bread they had spent all night baking. In the face of silence, the Riot Act was read, and Te Whiti and Tohu, those two wise birds, were arrested and gaoled in Christchurch and shown the error of their ways.

Over the next three weeks, Parihaka was torn down, crops were destroyed, houses were plundered for greenstone, women were assaulted and raped by troops, and many later gave birth. A rock still stands in the stream where they cleansed themselves.

Fifteen thousand people were evicted from their homes and left to wander the land in starvation, while others were employed to build fences across the land they had ploughed, yet still the Taranaki Māori refused to fight.

For a century, successive governments concealed the brutal truth behind the military destruction of Parihaka. The community was finally offered a formal apology in 2017, and while the British celebrate 5 November as Bonfire Night, Taranaki Māori remember *Te Rā o te Pāhua*, the Day of Plunder, and whenever people ask what happened, the reply is: 'Ask that mountain, Taranaki saw it all.'

A Māori girl from Taranaki went missing, and when she returned, she told the women in the *marae* that she was on the mountain with the Patupariarehe but escaped when the mist lifted. The women nudged each other and told her they had all run away with the Patupaiarehe when they were her age.

Time flows like a tidal river in Aotearoa, in a whirlpool of dreams and memories. Water is human here. In 2017, when the Whanganui River was poisoned with farm detritus, killing many fish, Māori persuaded the government to grant her the same legal rights and *mana* as people. Anyone hurting the river could be accused of manslaughter. Māori retain rights over their land, even when developers move in. The concept of indigenous land 'ownership' transcends signed contracts and electronic transfers. If anything, the land owns the people.

On 15 January 2019, I sat sketching an 800-year-old *rimu* tree in the ancient bush of Otari-Wilton's, which features in the illustration at the beginning of this chapter. It was alive when the giant eagle Pouakai hunted on Taranaki, before Māori learned to live peacefully alongside the Patupaiarehe, and over 500 years before Europeans brought rats, wars, possums, plagues and Hokey Pokey ice cream.

26

River Mumma

There is a fairy-tale castle in North Wales where no one in my family ever set foot. My father told me ogres lived there, and they were nastier than any I'd meet in a fairy tale. This was Castell Penrhyn, home to the owners of Bethesda Slate Quarry and the cause of a strike in 1900 that lasted three years and left bitterness so deep that many locals still won't go near it 120 years later, despite now being run by the National Trust. Folk memory is long and stubborn, and never forgets injustice.

Penrhyn was built around 200 years ago by the first Baron George Hay Dawkins-Pennant, on the ruins of an older Welsh castle using money from his sugar and rum businesses in Clarendon, Jamaica, where he enslaved over 600 people and was a leading supporter of slavery. A small township called Pennants now stands in the midst of his old plantations, where descendants of enslaved people still carry his name, and the North Wales Jamaica Society runs projects to make amends for their ancestor's cruelties.

In the Bog Walk Gorge in the neighbouring parish of St Catherine, enslaved people built the Flat Bridge over the Rio Cobre River to carry crops from the northern plantations to Kingston for export. Below the bridge lies a golden table, hidden beneath the murky waters like all the wealth in Jamaica. No one tries to steal it because they know they'll drown. Accidents happen here, caused by the ghosts of those who died during the construction of the bridge. Or maybe it's the *duppies*, the hidden people. Or that mysterious figure with a long tail who sits on a boulder and brushes her hair when the river turns lizard-green on moonlit nights, while her children, the *tiki tiki* fish and *janga* crayfish, swim around her.

River Mumma swam through the dark mirror from West Africa alongside the slave ships. In the famous poem by Lorna Goodison, she is weary of being a bridge between old and new Jamaica. She wants to be dancehall queen of the Caribbean, care for the rivers and the sea and maybe watch Chris Gayle hit sixes out of Sabina Park. So, she pulls the odd car off the bridge into the water, while the rest drive on to the wealthy resorts at Ocho Rios on the White River coast, where urban legends, online blogs and Jamaican patois tell this tale.

Elvis lived by the bridge over the White River in St Mary on the border with St Ann. His mother christened him after her hero, but Elvis reckoned he had the name first, and the king had never paid him a dollar in copyright. And he needed money to help his poor sick mama, and he knew the old story of how River Mumma had hidden some pirate gold by the bridge. So, Elvis decided to find the lost treasure.

He was sat by the pool on the river below his house, thinking there's no romance in being poor in Jamaica, when Gran'ma Hortense sat down beside him. Hortense was tall, white-haired and dark-skinned, a haunted old soul who'd never married yet had countless grandchildren and lived with her chickens in an old hut upriver. She enjoyed a good quarrel with Pastor Brathwaite, for she followed the old religion of *obeah*, carried a machete and invited young men into her bed. And Pastor Brathwaite was from Barbados, so they disagreed about cricket.

Elvis was suspicious that Hortense was an *ol' Higue*, who was going to suck his blood, or eat a baby, or turn into an owl, because that's what old hags do, or so mama said. But no, Hortense told him how to find the pirate gold. All he needed was River Mumma's comb, and then she would come to him in a dream and show him where the money was, and he'd cure mama.

Hortense gave him some apples, bananas and a coconut, he thanked her, and she loped off.

Now, most folk thought Elvis a dreamer, a *winjy*, a foo-fool, but he said, 'I'm going to find River Mumma's comb!' If only he knew where she lived.

He looked upriver where the water flowed fast from a cave into a waterfall then trickled into the quiet pool where he dived off a white rock to catch shrimps. He looked downriver where the water flowed fast beneath the bridge between St Mary and St Ann on its way to the big hotels they were building in Ocho Rios.

Elvis figured out that the mermaid lived in the cave upriver and at night hauled out on the white rock to comb her hair ready for a night out in Ochi. So, at Christmas, Elvis built himself a wooden hut on the riverbank overlooking River Mumma's rock, and he watched and waited.

Pastor Brathwaite called and told him that the mermaid was a folk belief from the old *obeah* religion, brought from Africa in the minds of slaves. She had no place in Christian Jamaica and Elvis should go home, look after his mama and come to church on Sunday.

Elvis said, 'I'll wait for River Mumma.'

Elvis's uncles and aunts visited and told him that the mermaid was a manatee, and even if she existed, the white-water rafters would have frightened her away, and they told him to go home to his sick mama.

Elvis said, 'I'll wait for River Mumma.'

Then the *duppies* came out of the forest and they didn't ask questions or tell him to go home, they burned his hut to the ground, and called him a foo-fool.

And the village agreed, 'That boy is a foo-fool.'

Elvis sat on the riverbank and watched the white rock while the frogs croaked and the crickets sang, and he thought, 'I'm little but I'm *tallawah*! I'm strong!'

At New Year he rebuilt his hut and waited for River Mumma.

The village and his family and the pastor and the duppies all agreed, 'That boy is a bigger foo-fool than we thought.'

All except Gran'ma Hortense.

One moonlit night, the air turned cool, and Elvis heard a splash. And there she was, sat on the great white rock, as dark as the night, her tail swishing in the moonlight, combing her long black hair.

Elvis waded into the mud at the water's edge and splashed around, 'River Mumma! River Mumma! It's me, Elvis. I'm not fraidy!'

River Mumma dived into the water and vanished. Elvis swam out to the rock, and there, shining in the moonlight, was her golden comb.

He took it to his mother's house, burst into her room, and shouted excitedly, 'Mama, you'll be well again.'

His mother said, 'What you talking about, Elvis?'

'Mama, look, I have the mermaid's golden comb!'

Mama looked at the comb. It was old and rusty and covered in weed, and it was tin, not gold. She shook her head, turned over and went to sleep.

That night Elvis slept in his own bed and he dreamed he saw River Mumma sat on the rock combing her hair, and she was angry. She told him that if he didn't give her comb back, she would pull his mama's house into the river. And she thrashed her tail until the house wobbled and tumbled down the bank.

Elvis woke up, sweating. That wasn't the dream he was supposed to have. He ran outside and saw that some of the land really had washed into the river. He had the same dream every night, and each morning when he ran outside, more land had washed away until the house was wobbling on the edge.

Pastor Brathwaite explained, 'Elvis, your father built this house, it's your mama's home. Give me the comb, turn from the old ways and come to church on Sunday!'

But Elvis said, 'I'll keep River Mumma's comb till she tells me where the treasure is.'

And the villagers said, 'You foo-fool, your mama won't have a house to live in when it falls into the river! Give the comb back to River Mumma!'

That night, Gran'ma Hortense sat down beside him on the riverbank. She gave him some apples and bananas and a coconut and told him to follow her. Elvis thought she was probably going to take him into her bed, but Hortense read his thoughts and laughed out loud. The night was black. No streetlamps, only the moon and stars and the *peenywallys*, the fireflies, to guide them along the muddy road. They squelched on until they came to the mermaid's cave, where Hortense left an offering and prayed to one of her gods.

'Don't worry, Elvis, we don't sacrifice young men anymore!' And oh how she laughed!

Come Sunday afternoon and the village had moved the furniture out of mama's house before it fell into the river, and there was Elvis stood on the bridge with the rusty old comb in his hand and Gran'ma Hortense by his side, and they said, 'There's foo-fool Elvis with Hortense the *ol' Higue*!'

Hortense nodded, and Elvis dropped the comb. As it hit the water, the house crumbled down the bank and washed away downriver.

And then they saw it. A great wooden trunk floating towards the bridge. They waded into the river, hauled it out and broke open the chains and gasped. Were they still in Elvis's dream? No, the pirate treasure had been buried under Elvis's house all along.

Well, Elvis paid a doctor to help his mother, then he built her a new house on the banks of the river and gave away the rest of the treasure to the people who called him a foo-fool. Elvis might have been poor, but he was no foo-fool, he was a god.

Dr Martin Luther King stayed in a rented house on the White River while he wrote his book, *Where Do We Go From Here: Chaos or Community?* Elvis went to visit to him, then kissed his mama goodbye and sailed from Kingston to London, and River Mumma swam beside him and lived beneath the bridges over the Thames. They're still there, the foo-fool and the mermaid, working tirelessly to bring justice to the Jamaicans who'd been invited by the British Government to rebuild the country in 1948, and found themselves in a 'hostile environment'.

27

The People Who Could Fly

GULLAH, GEECHEE

Long time ago, Buh Bear and Buh Tiger were walking through a swamp looking for food.

'My belly's rumbling,' said Buh Bear.

'Mine too,' said Buh Tiger, 'I could eat a whole man.'

Just then they saw an Igbo man carrying a fiddle in a bag. He was on his way to perform at a party, and he was so fine a fiddler that when he leaned back and drew the bow, all the people's feet started dancing. He looked round and saw Buh Bear and Buh Tiger following him.

'I'm gonna fill their bellies,' he thought.

'He's gonna fill my belly,' said Buh Bear.

'No, he's gonna fill my belly,' said Buh Tiger.

Well, the man ran, and Buh Tiger and Buh Bear chased him, so he flew up a tree and sat on a branch. 'Now I won't fill their bellies,' said the man.

'Now how'm I gonna fill my belly?' said Buh Bear, 'I can't fly up a tree,'

'You're not. I'm gonna fill my belly,' said Buh Tiger, and he started to climb the tree.

The man took his fiddle out of the bag and drew the bow and played, and Buh Tiger's feet started dancing all on their own and he fell out of the tree. Buh Bear grabbed him, and they started jiving, and the faster the fiddler played, the faster they danced, round and round till they fell to the ground and couldn't get up again. The fiddler flew out of the tree to the party where he was performing, and Buh Tiger and Buh Bear hadn't the strength to follow.

'My belly's rumbling,' said Buh Bear.

'Mine too,' said Buh Tiger, 'I'm gonna get that Igbo man.'

This story is from the Igbo oral storytelling tradition in Nigeria, yet it was written down by a white man, Charles Colcock Jones Jr, the Mayor of Savannah, Georgia, who heard it from the enslaved people on his family's cotton plantation. They told it in *Gullah Geechee*, a shared creole language from the Atlantic coast of Georgia, Virginia and the Carolinas, that allowed people from different parts of Africa to understand each other and hide their words from traders like Bear and Tiger. It was the language of oral storytelling when there was no written word.

My friend Phil Okwedy tells Welsh Nigerian stories, and it was from him that I heard the tale of around seventy-five Igbo people who, in May 1803, landed on St Simons Island, Glynn County, Georgia, on board the slave ship *Wanderer*. They were offered for sale at around $100 each, packed into a coastal boat, the *York*, and sold to local plantations.

During the short voyage along the coast, they escaped at Dunbar Creek, now known as Igbo Landing. They sang to the water spirits and waded into the sea. Roswell King, a white overseer on the nearby Pierce Butler plantation, discovered thirteen bodies and later wrote the story down. But he didn't know all the story. The rest of the people had flown home to Nigeria.

Henry 'Box' Brown was born in 1815 on Hermitage plantation in Louisa County, Virginia, and by 1849 he was married with three children. His wife Nancy was expecting another child when her master sold her, even though Henry had been paying him not to. Henry knew African conjuring and stage magic, he could pick up a nail, close his hand, speak creole words and when he opened his hand, the nail turned into an acorn that would grow into a nail tree. Henry was a trickster, and he could fly.

On 23 March 1849, he poured sulphuric acid over his hand to get the day off work. With the help of black freedman 'Boxer' Smith and $83 saved from selling tobacco, he squeezed into a small wooden box lined with baize, containing a few biscuits, a bottle of water and an awl to bore air-holes, and posted himself via the Adams

Express Company to the Quaker merchant Passmore Williams of the Philadelphia Vigilance Committee.

During his flight from slavery, Henry's box was transported by wagon, railroad, steamboat and ferry for twenty-seven hours, sometimes upside down with blood rushing to his head.

He arrived safely in Philadelphia on 24 March 1849 and shortly afterwards he published his autobiography, *Narrative of the Life of Henry 'Box' Brown.* Henry built another box, open at the front like a picture frame, with a handle on top that turned a long, illustrated scroll. It was a moving panorama, like a picture book or an animated film, a tradition of visual storytelling called a 'crankie' in Virginia, Appalachia and Wales. It was huge, taller than a person, with forty-nine scenes painted onto a canvas scroll by the ornamental sign painter and abolitionist Josiah Wolcott. It told the history of his people, and Henry called it, 'Mirror of Slavery'.

He premiered it in Boston in April 1850 to large crowds and great acclaim from newspaper reviewers. But that summer, the Fugitive Slave Bill passed, and Henry was attacked in Providence. It was time to fly again, so in October he sailed for Liverpool on the packet ship *Constantine* with 'Boxer' Smith and his moving panorama.

He settled in Stockport near Manchester, where he published a new edition of his book, which introduced his story to a wider audience. Within the year, he filled theatres throughout the north of England, advertising himself as 'King of all the Mesmerisers', 'Professor of Animal-magnetism' and 'Doctor of Electro-Biology'.

On 22 May 1852, ever the showman, Henry packed himself into a box the size of the one he had escaped in and was paraded through Leeds to the Music Hall in Albion Street, where he freed himself on stage, did handkerchief and card tricks, vanished through mirrors and boxes, escaped from chained sacks like Houdini and introduced his audience to the oral history of slavery through visual storytelling.

In 1855 he married Jane Brown from Copperhouse in Cornwall. Their daughter Agnes was born in Stockport and they moved to Keighley, where they had a son, Edward. In November 1863, Henry gave a final performance of 'Mirror of Slavery' in Cardiff, though he returned to Wales two years later with new panoramas like 'Diorama of the Holy Land' and gave gifts to the audience in the Temperance Hall in Merthyr Tydfil, although in Aberdare, 'the attendance was not large'.

By 1871, the family returned to Cheetham Hill in Manchester, not far from the hidden people of Boggart Hole Clough. After touring for twenty-five years, the Browns migrated to America. Henry, now a free man, performed his panoramas in Canada till his final flight to his God in Toronto in 1897.

☙❦❧

Most maroons, escaped slaves, did not have the support Henry received, nor his extraordinary imagination and entrepreneurial skills as a performance artist. One of the scenes in his moving panorama was of the great Dismal Swamp in North Carolina, a hiding place for maroons who used oral storytelling as a secret library of defiance, freedom and flight.

Between the Great Dismal Swamp and Igbo Landing is Roanoke Island on the Outer Banks of North Carolina, where Sir Walter Raleigh brought an early colony of Europeans in 1585. A year later, the privateer and pirate Sir Francis Drake also landed on Roanoke, rescued the settlers from their war with the native people and left behind his cargo of African Jamaican and Colombian slaves.

Raleigh returned the following year with more settlers, including the mother of the soon-to-be-born Virginia Dare. The slaves had vanished and, shortly after, so did the new settlers. To celebrate Virginia's 350th birthday in 1937, a play was commissioned and performed outdoors near Manteo on Roanoke Island, which told the story of *The Lost Colony* with a cast of predominantly white actors playing Sir Walter, Queen Elizabeth and stereotypical native people. The play is still performed annually. I saw it in 2019, and the lost enslaved people are not mentioned. Written out of history.

Across Roanoke Sound is Kill Devil Hills, where a museum and memorial commemorate the spot where on 17 December 1903, Wilbur and Orville Wright, two bicycle makers from Dayton, Ohio, believed they were the first folks to fly. However, oral Black history tells that people flew from the Gullah Geechee lands almost

100 years earlier, though it's a difficult story for those who adhere to rational thought.

A young woman is picking cotton in the field, carrying her newborn baby on her back, when she stumbles from exhaustion in the hot sun. The overseer whips her and tells her to get back to work. The baby cries, so she throws her breast over her shoulder and sings lullabies in Gullah. He whips her again, this time for singing, and her baby, too.

They are weak now, so the woman asks for help from the oldest enslaved man on the plantation. He tells her to stay strong. The young woman falls again and is whipped for the third time. She turns to the old man, and he tells her to stand. She straightens her back, lifts her head into the air and she and her baby take to the sky and fly away from the plantation like leaves blown in the wind. The slaveholders run after her, but too late. The blackbird has flown.

The overseer orders the people to get back to work, but a male slave falls from exhaustion and he too is whipped. He looks at the old man who speaks to him in Gullah. The overseer tells the man to work, but he stands tall, laughs in their faces, and flies away after the young woman.

Another slave falls from weakness, the old man speaks, and she flies away too. The overseer realises the old man is responsible for this and orders him to be whipped, but the old man speaks in Gullah, lifts his arms, and releases a secret that reminds the enslaved folk who were born in Africa of the magic they know.

Flying is like climbing a tree when you know the magic, and they take off, a flock of blackbirds against the blue sky. And what a sight it is, young and old, women with babies at their breasts, grandmas who can barely walk, chasing the horizon back to their homes in Africa.

The people born on the plantation watch and fear for their lives because they don't know the words and have never been taught how to fly. One day they will learn, and they will fly across invisible borders and tell their children how they became free as birds, like the flying Africans.

In 1940, the Savannah Unit of the Federal Writers' Project interviewed 134 African Americans from the Georgia and Carolina coast about their lives and published them as *Drums and Shadows*. The people made no distinction between the magical and earthly worlds. Transmigration was as real as walking.

James Moore had watched people disappear in front of his eyes. Rosa Grant spoke of how her mother, with two quick swings of her skirt, took to the air with her gran watching. Caesar Grant, former slave of St John's Island, South Carolina, knew a group on a plantation who leapt into the air with a shout and blew away like a handful of leaves over the fields and fences beyond the horizon. Former slave Jack Wilson said they had magic that could fly them back to Africa. Martha Page, former slave of Yamacraw near Savannah, said her grandfather knew the 'strange talk' the Africans spoke. Prince Sneed's grandmother taught him the words:

> *Kum buba yali kum buba tambe, Kum kunka yali kum kunka tambe.*

Similar to a Luba proverb, which translates as:

> He is tricky, I will win by being tricky too, he asks smart questions, I will win by asking smarter ones.

That's what the old trickster Henry 'Box' Brown did, too.

28

The Woman Who Fell in Love
With a Pumpkin

འབྲུག་ཡུལ, BHUTAN, NEW HAMPSHIRE

A few years ago, I spent an evening singing with the sacred
harp choir at the Helen Hills Chapel at Smith College in
Northampton, Massachusetts. The harmonies that wove
round that vast echoing chamber heightened the senses to such a
degree that when I stepped into the dense New England night, I'd
time-slipped into another world.

I walked 6 miles through the darkness to John Clapp's farm near
Florence, where I was staying, carefully avoiding the *pukwudgies*, the
little people who play tricks on confused travellers. I slept that night
in John's forest, in a red-painted replica of Henry David Thoreau's
writing cabin from nearby Concord, New Hampshire, where he
wrote *Walden* and meditated on solitude, silence and nature. Even
the bed, chair, writing desk and window lights were facsimiles of
Thoreau's, as was the sense of isolation, although the real cabin at
Concord was close enough to the town that his mother brought
him clean laundry and Sunday lunch every week.

At daybreak, I found out why John told me not to leave the
cabin until he fetched me. Sat on the porch was old trickster coyote,
staring hungrily at the window like the lean feral dogs he interbreeds
with. He ran off when John appeared in the clearing with a plate
of blueberry pancakes, pumpkin pie and a jug of maple syrup. We
shared yarns at Thoreau's replica table as the forest awoke, wood-
peckers yaffled, time slowed and seasons blurred.

The following day I caught the Vermonter over the border into
New Hampshire heading towards White River Junction. The
Amtrak trundled so slowly along the banks of the Connecticut
River it was overtaken by a bald eagle, who turned its white head
dismissively towards the passengers. It was on this journey I heard
a strange story that Thoreau told in *A Week on the Concord and*

Merrimack Rivers in 1849. Though it really began with Cotton Mather, the New England puritan scientist who wrote *Memorable Providences*, the book that inspired the Salem Witch Trials of 1692 and who, ten years later, published the true tale of Hannah Duston.

She was born Hannah Emerson in 1657 and lived in Haverhill, not far from John Clapp's Farm in Florence. On 15 March 1697, Haverhill was attacked by a group of Abenaki looking for children and women to replace those killed by the colonists or European diseases. Twenty-seven settlers died. Hannah was taken hostage along with her nurse Mary Neff, while her husband Thomas Duston escaped with six of their children, although their newborn baby Martha was captured and her head dashed against an apple tree to stop her crying.

Duston and Neff were taken north across the border into New Hampshire, and given to a Pennacook family of two men, three women and seven children along with 14-year-old Samuel Leonardson, an English boy who had been taken a year earlier from Worcester, Massachusetts.

One night, they were camped by Beaver Lake near Derry, when a native fairy woman emerged from the water, introduced herself as Tsienneto, and told Duston she would help.

Tsienneto followed the party north along the Merrimack River to Thoreau's Concord. They camped on Sugar Ball Island at the confluence with the Contoocook River, where Tsienneto cast a spell over the natives, aided by a sleeping draft added to the soup by Duston.

On the night of 30 March, while the family slept, Duston, Neff and Leonardson killed and scalped four adults and six children, while an injured older woman and a small boy escaped. Tsienneto helped the settlers paddle a birch-bark canoe back down the white-water rapids of the Merrimack to safety, where the General Assembly of Massachusetts paid them £50 for the scalps. The names of the dead natives, the old woman and the small boy were not recorded.

To Cotton Mather, Hannah Duston was a folk heroine, a brave white woman who killed ten 'savages'. He never mentioned Tsienneto, for he viewed the supernatural in the same way as natives, witches, Catholics and the French, as 'others'.

Thoreau took a more enlightened view, in keeping with his sympathies towards native people and their deeper connection to the river as a stream of consciousness and home to woodpecker, beaver and muskrat. He visited the Duston homestead in 1850 and walked in her footsteps but found only holes in the ground and burned-out houses, and no apple tree. Curiously, he never mentioned Tsienneto either.

The 'Legend of Tsienneto' was first published in 1945 when Eva A. Speare included it in her book of *New Hampshire Folk Tales*, as told by Mrs J.G. MacMurphy of Derry, a descendent of the first settlers along the Merrimack River. She is remembered in Derry, too, where the track to her home in Beaver Lake is named Tsienneto Road.

Mrs Duston is memorialised as a statue on Sugar Ball Island, dressed in an off-the-shoulder gown, holding a tomahawk in one hand and a fistful of human scalps in the other, a disturbing reminder of the way First Nations people have been stereotyped and abused. In an attempt at redress, the memorial site has been renamed *N'dakinna*, 'our land' in Abenaki.

In the 1990s, more settlers came to New Hampshire. They were Nepali-speaking farmers and herders from Bhutan who had been sent to refugee camps by the Buddhist government, who had ironically introduced a policy to promote gross national happiness.

Hari Tiwari had tended the cows and goats on her parents' farm in Dumfa before the family were moved to the UN Beldangi Two Camp in Nepal, where they lived for eighteen years. When they arrived in frozen New Hampshire in 2008, Hari remembered a version of this traditional tale from Bhutan being told by her father to the elders in the Oxfam school, while he combed her long hair.

A woman and her husband worked hard on their farm, where they tended the cows and goats, grew rice, corn, cucumbers, peas, beans, lentils and potatoes. One day, the woman made 100 dumplings, sat down, wiped her brow and said, 'I'm so tired. If I only had a child to take these dumplings to my husband in the maize field.'

'I'll help you, Amma.'

'Who said that?'

'Me. Your son.'

'I don't have a son.'

A pumpkin rolled out in front of her and spoke. 'Yes, that's me. I'll take the dumplings to father.'

Mother thought, 'I don't remember giving birth to a pumpkin.'

Pumpkin-boy pushed the dumplings into the field.

'Who are you?' asked the old man.

'Your son,' said pumpkin-boy.

'I don't have a son.'

'Yes, that's me.'

Father thought, 'My wife must have slept with a pumpkin!'

Pumpkin-boy rolled back to the house and said, 'Amma, I want to marry.'

Mother laughed and said, 'No one would marry a pumpkin.'

'Please, Amma, help me find a wife.'

'Well, the king in the neighbouring country has seven daughters, one of them might marry you. Just don't get your hopes up!'

Father came home and asked, 'Amma, have you slept with a pumpkin?'

Pumpkin-boy left his parents arguing and rolled over the border into the neighbouring land. He came to a big city and went to a great tall tower where the king lived. The King took one look at him, 'Is it Halloween already?'

'No sir, I'm from the Pumpkingdom. Please could I marry one of your daughters?'

The King thought he might make a profit trading with Pumpkingdom, so he called his oldest girl, but she said, 'I'm not marrying an orange vegetable!'

The King asked another, but she said, 'I'm not marrying a green-haired vegetable!'

None of his daughters wanted to marry pumpkin-boy, until the youngest said, 'I'll marry him. I like green hair, and he's not a vegetable, he's a fruit.'

So, youngest daughter dyed her hair green and married her Pumpkin Prince, who thought he was the luckiest pumpkin in the world. The king gave them a farm, where they tended the cows and goats, grew rice, corn, cucumbers, peas, beans, lentils and potatoes.

One day, the king sent them to Pumpkingdom to hold out the hand of friendship and set up some profitable trade deals. On the way, youngest daughter wove some *guhenla* flowers into a garland and placed it round her husband's neck. So, he climbed a tree to pick her some mangoes, but he fell off the branch onto a rock and smashed into pieces. As she cradled his squishy head and dried his lips, out of the pumpkin stepped a young man.

'Who are you?'

'I'm your husband. I thought you'd like me better this way. Look, I have all the requisite parts.'

'No, I liked you as you were.' And she pushed him back into the pumpkin and pieced him back together.

They went to pumpkin-boy's house, where his parents were still arguing. 'You have shamed me by sleeping with a pumpkin!' said father.

'I didn't sleep with a pumpkin. I would have remembered,' replied mother.

'Well, how did you give birth to a pumpkin-boy?'

'You have pumpkin DNA. Maybe your grandmother slept with a pumpkin?'

'No, Grandmother was a Buddhist.'

'You're in love with a courgette!'

'You've been to bed with a butternut squash!'

Pumpkin-boy interrupted and introduced his parents to his new bride, and they were so surprised he had found a wife who wasn't a fruit or vegetable, they stopped arguing and embraced their new daughter-in-law.

And Pumpkin-boy took all the pumpkins from his parents' farm back to his adopted country, where he sold them all profitably on Halloween.

And that's the story of the New England Pumpkin King.

Hari Tiwari's version of this old tale was published in 2013 as a children's book, *The Story of a Pumpkin: A Traditional Tale from Bhutan*, by the New Hampshire Humanities Project, based in Henry David Thoreau's old hometown of Concord. A book seems a more fitting memorial than a statue for a girl who never went to school and lived in a refugee camp for eighteen years, before finding a new life in the new land of New Hampshire.

29

Appalachian Mister Fox

APPALACHIA

In 2019, Appalachian folklorist and broadcaster Caitlin Tan noticed that the coal town of Fayetteville in West Virginia had been invaded by gnomes, resembling the English-garden variety or the Scandinavian *tomte*, mostly male with long white beards and pointy hats. They seemed in keeping with a land settled by Europeans, although it was actually a plot by the under-employed tourist authority to attract visitors, in the way the Icelandic economy had been rejuvenated by the reinvention of elves ten years earlier.

Appalachia comprises all of West Virginia and parts of Pennsylvania, North Carolina, Alabama, Georgia, Kentucky and Tennessee. It may not have geographical boundaries, but Appalachia has a unique cultural identity born of diversity and based on folk arts, mountain music and tall-tale-telling. European migrants came as coal miners, farmers and loggers, and brought enslaved people whose descendants developed a unique Affrilachian culture alongside the Eastern Band of the Cherokee, whose ancestors remained after the ethnic cleansings in the 1830s.

And there are Appalachians who defy stereotypes, like the residents of East Jackson, Ohio, raised to identify as black despite having white skin, and the Kentucky Blue People, descended from the family of Martin Fugate and Elizabeth Smith of Hazard and Troublesome Creek, who carried genes that caused subsequent generations to turn blue.

A few years ago, while visiting my own family in the old Welsh coal city of Morgantown, West Virginia, I spoke to several former miners in their nineties who had settled in Scott's Run as children. All considered themselves Appalachian American rather than Greek, German or Scots, underlining the idea that it takes three generations for migrant families to create an identity in a new homeland. Recently, the abandoned shopping malls, barn quilts, and microbreweries have begun to define an imaginative ever-changing community that has reclaimed

the derogatory term 'hillbilly' and uses art to distance themselves
from being seen as the forgotten poor.

To celebrate our shared cultures, I organised an exhibition of
Appalachian and Welsh folk art at Monongalia Arts Center in
downtown Morgantown. Caitlin Tan wrote, 'The exhibit is one big
story that contains many little stories, it is a bit like a fairy-tale book
come to life.' Which was exactly what I had hoped it would be.

So here is the tale of Appalachian Mister Fox, a story more familiar from England and the French Bluebeard that made itself at home
in the mountain states. It comes from the telling of Polly Johnson of
Norton, Virginia, and R.M. Ward of Beech Creek, North Carolina,
pieced together by folklorist Richard Chase in 1956. Even the
great Beech Mountain storyteller Ray Hicks learned tales from Mr
Chase's books. And I've added a children's rhyme and a few anec-
dotes from *Green Hills of Magic* and *Mountain Mother Goose*, Ruth
Ann Musick's classic collections of European folktales and rhymes
in West Virginia.

On Love I sit
On Love I stand
Love I hold within my hand
I see Love
Love don't see me
I see Love in yonder tree

A young girl called Polly told that riddle, and everyone called her
Pretty Polly after the old song. She came to Appalachia when she
was a girl and learned English, and now her folks were dead she
lived all alone, kept a few chickens and goats, grew squash and blue-
berries in her vegetable patch and played an old harmonium on the
porch.

One day, a stranger came courting, a slick-salesman of a feller,
said his name was Fox, and he invited her to meet him the following
Saturday beneath the old pine tree on the ridge.

Come Saturday, something felt wrong. Maybe this man was a city boy, sold real estate or cure-alls, or he was a photographer sent by the government to take pictures of poor folks. Or he was one of those troublesome little folk. Women were always going missing, but Polly could handle herself if he tried anything, so she dressed herself up and off she went. It was cold and the wind was blowing, and she was about to get out when she heard footsteps. She shimmied up the old pine tree and hid in the thickest branches.

She looked down and saw Mister Fox carrying a lantern. He brought out a shovel and started digging a hole, 6ft wide and 6ft deep, and Polly knew this grave was hers. The old pine tree blew sideways in the wind, and she was frozen, but Foxy looked like a wild animal down there, so she clung on until she heard a rooster crow and he took his shovel and left. When he was good and gone, she set off home and warmed herself by the stove.

That week, she overheard the townsfolk talking about three young women who'd disappeared. Mister Fox had been courting all three of them, but he never came to their houses and no one knew where he lived. Seems they'd all met him under that old pine tree. Polly set to thinking.

She'd heard about an old miner in Clarksburg whose Romanian uncle, Robert Capak, had married a bloodsucker from Transylvania. A Scots-Irish family told her to watch out for the Kunkitchy Man, who'd catch her if she picked flowers in the forest. And there were tommy knockers who'd come from Cornwall and caused floods and explosions in the mines. Maybe Foxy was one of these.

One day, Mister Fox stood on Polly's doorstep, and he spoke as smooth and slick as a medicine-show man. 'Would you do me the honour of walking out with me, Miss Polly?'

'Might, might not.'

'Come on, don't be shy.'

'I ain't shy, I got errands to run.'

'Saturday?'

'Where d'you live?'

'I'll come calling for you.'

'No, if I come, I'll call at yours.'

Fox said, 'Give me a sack of flour and I'll lay a trail. Follow it, you'll find me.'

As he left, he scattered a handful of flour every few footsteps behind him.

Polly didn't meet him that week, but the following Saturday inquisitiveness got the better of her. She followed the trail of flour till she came to a rickety old cabin in the middle of the wood. She hid behind a tree and waited till Mister Fox came out and headed off down the path. Then she crept inside.

A parrot hung in a cage in the doorway.'

'Don't go in there, Pretty Polly! You'll lose your heart's blood!'

'Sssh, polly parrot,' she said, with her finger to her mouth.

She went upstairs, opened a door and went inside. Well, it was like a slaughterhouse. Women hanging from the walls with their heads on the floor beneath them. Blood and guts everywhere. She felt sick and angry, but she kept calm, closed the door and ran downstairs and was about to leave when she heard a scream. She looked out the window and there was Foxy dragging a woman by the arm.

'Hide, Pretty Polly!' said the parrot, 'Hide!'

She hid under the rickety stairs.

'Shush, polly parrot. Don't tell him I'm here.'

'No, Pretty Polly. No!'

Mister Fox dragged the woman inside and up the stairs but she grabbed hold of the stair rail and bit him and he couldn't move her. He took out his knife and hacked her hand clean off. The hand fell through the cracks in the steps and landed in Polly's lap.

Fox smelled the air, and asked the parrot, 'Has anyone been here?'

'No, sir. No!'

He dragged the woman into the slaughter room and shut the door. There was a scream and then silence. Polly picked up the hand and touched the fingers. They moved. She ran for her life.

Well, that week, Polly watched Foxy like a swamp hawk to make sure he was up to no more trouble, while she hatched a plan. No use going to the sheriff, he was in the pay of the wealthy folks, and they didn't care about poor women.

Saturday evening, there was a party in the settlement, with dancing and moonshine and kissing games. The girls told their dreams and asked riddles round the fire and scared each other with ghost stories. Polly saw Mister Fox through the crowd, looking this way and that.

She sat by the fire and listened to the old folks who were tellin', and when it came to her turn, she said, 'I've got a riddle.'

'Go on, Pretty Polly, tell us.'

Riddle to my riddle to my right
Where was I that Saturday night?
All that time in a lonesome pine
I was high and he was low
The cock did crow the wind did blow,
The tree did shake and my heart did ache
to see what a hole that fox did make.

Well, they guessed and guessed, and all the while Mister Fox sat there.

'Tell us, tell us?'

'I'll tell, but first I'll tell a weird dream I had the other night.'

'Ain't no truth in dreams,' said Fox.

But the folks begged her, 'Tell us, Pretty Polly.'

Polly folded her arms under her apron. 'I dreamed I followed Mister Fox to his house. He wasn't home, but he'd invited me, so I went in, and his old polly parrot said, "Don't go in, Pretty Polly! You'll lose your heart's blood!" Inside was a slaughter-room with women hangin' on the walls, all cut up.'

'No!' said Fox, but all eyes were on him. They knew women had gone missing.

'I dreamed I heard a woman scream, and in came Foxy draggin' her behind.'

'No!' said Fox.'

A couple of men moved to the door and blocked it.

'I dreamed that polly parrot told me to hide under the stairs, the woman grabbed hold of the stair rail and Mr Fox took out his knife and hacked her hand clean off.'

Fox leapt up, and said:

It was not so,
And it is not so

And God forbid,
It ever should be so.

More folks went to the door to stop Fox leaving.

Polly continued, 'Then I dreamed he dragged the poor woman into the slaughter room and there was a blood-curdlin' scream. I ran, fearin' I'd be next.'

It was not so,
And it is not so
And God forbid,
It ever should be so.

Polly took a cotton cloth from under her apron, unwrapped it and held the hand in front of Foxy's nose.

But it was so,
And it is so
And here's the bloody hand to show!

The men grabbed hold of Foxy and he was kicking and squealing like a pig when they dragged him to the jail, shouting about how all those women weren't pure white like him and deserved what they got.

And that's how the daughter of a migrant used a riddle and a story to lock Mister Fox behind bars where he belonged.

On Love I sit
On Love I stand
Love I hold within my hand
I see Love
Love don't see me
I see Love in yonder tree

30

Cherokee Little People
(Yunwi Tsunsdi)

ᎠᏂᏳᏂᏫ, CHEROKEE

In September 2015, the eight Warriors of AniKituwha appeared on one of the main stages at the National Folk Festival in Greensboro, North Carolina, in their role as cultural ambassadors of the Eastern Band of the Cherokee. They performed the Friendship Dance, the Buffalo Dance, the Eagle Tail Dance, the Beaver Hunting Dance and the War Dance.

The warriors were joined on stage during the Bear Dance by children and grown-ups from the predominantly white audience who learned how to be grizzlies. A little girl asked Bo Taylor, storyteller and spokesman, what the dance meant, and he replied, 'Hey, we just like being bears.'

Afterwards, Bo was approached by a lady with two children, who asked about his life. He explained he lived in a house and had kids like hers. She looked quizzically at his body paint, loincloth and naked belly and said, 'Oh no, not like mine,' and scurried away, arms around her children.

Storytelling and the folk arts help explain the cultural identity of the Eastern Cherokee to an America that persists in seeing them as from another world. In the introduction to her book of oral *Stories of the Yunwi Tsunsdi: The Cherokee Little People* in 1991, Jeannie Reed writes that stories don't begin in the European way with 'Once upon a time', but rather with, 'When I was little …' or 'This happened to …' These are not folk tales, but first-hand encounters with the mischievous little people of the Great Smoky Mountains in Southern Appalachia, and Tahlequah in the foothills of the Ozarks in north-west Oklahoma.

Back in the late 1800s, the medicine man A`yûn'inï' (Swimmer), told stories of the little people to the Smithsonian ethnologist James

Mooney. A`yûn'inï' explained they were no taller than a person's knee and lived in nests scooped out of sand and covered in dry grass.

One day, the wind blew white feathers across the land and a great cloud of white geese flew up from the south. The geese poked their long beaks into the little people's nests and pecked at them, so they asked the Cherokee for help. The Cherokee taught them how to defend themselves with clubs and hit the geese on their necks till they flew away. All was well until a great cloud of tall sandhill cranes with longer beaks came and gobbled them all up.

A`yûn'inï' said they were no higher than a person's knee, though some could be taller, and they looked after the forest, helped passing travellers, warned of impending war, turned invisible at will, teleported from place to place and lived forever. They built elaborate townhouses under mountains, where they cared for injured humans. One lies beneath Blood Mountain in Georgia, another under Pilot Knob in Powell County, Kentucky, and below the Nikwasi mound in downtown Franklin, North Carolina. These 2,000-year-old mounds are all over the Eastern Cherokee lands around the Great Smoky Mountains, where the little people hid from settlers and invaders.

Mooney was told a story by Itagunuhi (John Ax) about a hunter who was tracking a black bear in the Great Smoky mountains, but no matter how many arrows he fired, they bounced off its thick fur. He realised this was a medicine bear and remembered that west of the Oconaluftee River was the mystical medicine lake of Atagâ'hï that no human eye had seen, where the bears bathed their wounds in its enchanted waters.

Many hunters had followed bear tracks in search of it but all they found was a dry lakebed. Had they stayed till daybreak, they would have seen the cracked ground fill with purple water, fish and reptiles, till the lake was covered with flocks of coloured waterfowl.

The hunter stopped firing arrows and thought to himself, 'This bear will kill me.'

The bear heard his thoughts, and spoke, 'No, I won't hurt you.'

The man's belly rumbled with hunger.

The bear heard. 'Come with me, I'll feed you.'

So, the hunter followed the bear to a large cave full of old bears, young bears, white bears, black bears and brown bears. They were holding a council to discuss the scarcity of food in the mountains when two bears returned from foraging in a valley knee deep in berries, nuts and acorns. The bears danced in celebration of the feast that awaited them.

The black bear took the hunter to his own cave, where she sat up on her hind legs, rubbed her stomach, held out her forepaws and offered the hunter chestnuts, huckleberries, blackberries and acorns, and soon his belly was full. They lived together through the winter and come spring, the hunter was as hairy as his friend, though he still walked like a man.

He remembered the story of a hunter named Tsantäwû', who had disappeared in the mountains at the head of the Oconaluftee River during a cold winter in the late 1800s. The little people found him, his legs frozen to his knees, so they took him to their cave, fed him on large loaves that shrunk into small cakes, and after sixteen days when the weather improved, they led him to a shallow creek. When he crossed over and looked back to thank them, the Yunwi tsunsdi had vanished, and the creek was a deep, wide river.

Come spring, more hunters came up the mountain and found the cave. They set their dogs on the bear, stripped the fur from her body and cut her up for meat. They found the hairy hunter cowering in the cave and thought he was another bear, until he spoke Tsalagi. The hunters recognised him as their lost friend and took him back to the village, but before he left, he piled leaves over the spot where the bear had been skinned and, as he looked back, she rose out of the leaves, shook herself and disappeared into the woods.

Back at the village the hunter was isolated for seven days without food so he would lose his bear nature and become a man again. Then his wife took him home, but it was too soon, and he stayed a bear till the day he died.

The Yunwi tsunsdi are still around. Jeannie Reed interviewed people at the Tsalla Manor Nursing Home on the Qualla Boundary in 1991, where Elder Bessie Jumper said they lived under her house in the Snowbird Mountains of North Carolina, which is home to a whole heap of little people. They rattled the pipes, though she didn't mind because no one would dare rob a house where the little people lived.

Elder Al Lossiah's mother was of the Deer Clan, and she said there were three kinds of little folk who lived there. The Rock People were mean and stole children and taught them to know their boundaries, the Laurel People played tricks and pinched children to make them laugh and taught them not to take life too seriously, while the Dogwood People just took care of folks and taught them not to expect anything in return.

In 1838, the Cherokee were evicted from their Appalachian homeland under the Indian Removal Act and around 12,000 people were marched in winter under military guard over 800 miles from the Great Smoky Mountains through the Ozarks to Oklahoma. This was the ethnic cleansing known as The Trail Where They Cried. Black enslaved people walked alongside, and so did the little people, who offered comfort and protection and kept an everlasting fire alight through wind, snow and rain, as a symbol of hope and a memory of the old beliefs. Those who survived found themselves in a strange land, forgotten and displaced, as invisible as the little people.

Writer Betty Lombardi wrote of an Oklahoma man called Wilson Angle, who kept two little people, a boy and a girl, in stone milk jars out east of his house to protect his property from being stolen. Angle fed them nothing but 'straight water corn bread', and when he died they went to live with Buster Stone in the same neighbourhood.

Lombardi also told of a 90-year-old medicine woman who said the little folk made a path on the west side of her house and came each evening for food, until a waterline was installed that blocked their visits. The little people love to hang around medicine folk, so they can help with chores and make mischief when they get bored.

Robert Conley wrote that one afternoon in the early twenty-first century, medicine man John Little Bear was at home on Stick Ross Mountain outside Tahlequah, Oklahoma, and he was looking for something. He called it by name, frowned and said, 'Those danged little people. They're always hiding things from me.' If Little Bear found anything he wanted in the woods, say some berries or a knife, he had to say something like, 'Little People, I'm taking these berries and this knife', and then he left some whisky outside his cabin for them, though they were more partial to local honeycomb. They taught Little Bear a song to call them up if he needed help and he would ask them to go to the homes of troubled folks to help him fight the bad medicine.

But dang it, he never could find whatever it was he was looking for.

Another hidden people were the slaves kept by wealthier Cherokee. Some were natives from tribes defeated in battle, while others were black freedmen, an inconvenient truth that has caused division for many years. Black Cherokee storyteller Tony Hopkins writes:

> My ancestors were both African slaves and natives of the New World.
> People stolen from their land and a people who had their land
>   stolen from them.
> Never disconnected from one and not quite connected to the other.
> Of Africa, not African. Born in America not American.
> There's no identity problem, only a problem of identity.

31

We're Still Here

Dxʷdəwʔabš, DUWAMISH

Amongst the art galleries, intolerance-friendly cafés and London plane trees of Occidental Park in Seattle's Pioneer Square district stand totem poles built by Alaskan artist and teacher Duane Pasco to remind passers-by of the conflicts between worlds. One is of Tsonoqua, the bringer of fever dreams, invoked by exasperated parents to frighten their children to sleep, while the other is Bear, the strong and powerful medicine animal who protects people from their worst nightmares. Below the square is another land, a hidden underworld of streets, buildings and people.

Old Seattle was built on tideland that frequently flooded, with sewers that overflowed following the regular rains and earthquakes. After a devastating fire in 1889, the wealthy city elders financed constructors to raise the roads to the height of first floor level. For a few years, people walked around on pavements several metres below the traffic and climbed ladders at street corners to cross the roads.

The remains of the old pavements, shops and houses that used to be at ground level are still there beneath the car-stuffed streets, and they carry a dark secret. The city was built on sin.

In 1853, two years after Seattle was settled by Europeans on land where the Duwamish and Suquamish had lived for generations, Mary Conklin arrived from Philadelphia to become landlady of the fledgling city's first inn. Mary's ability to swear in six languages came in useful in this frontier world, particularly when she opened a brothel above the courthouse, earning her the title 'Madame Damnable'. Some of the sex workers at this time were native women, forced to search for jobs in the settlers' world after the loss of their land and the betrayal of the Treaty of Point Elliott.

By the time Madame Lou Graham arrived from Germany in 1888, the city economy was established on prostitution, although the backlash had begun, with the revoking of liquor licences and the mass closure of brothels. Following the 1889 fire, Lou persuaded

a local bank to finance the construction of a four-storey red-brick Romanesque building in Pioneer Square named the Washington Court House. It was a high-class establishment with prices comparable to the finest hotels, free alcohol for city elders and a select staff who could discuss the arts, politics and economics with their business clients.

Lou and her girls were officially described as 'seamstresses', which gave them an air of respectability, protected the regulars and hid them from Puritan eyes. Soon, more business transactions took place at Lou's than the city hall a few blocks away.

When she was charged with licentious behaviour in 1892, Lou was represented in court by a judge and a senator, found not guilty and the city mayor was forced to resign. By the time the Klondike Gold Rush boomed in 1897, Lou was a major landowner in the city. When she died six years later, aged 46, she left her estate to her family in Germany, but the city fathers appropriated it and built modern Seattle on the wealth of a woman they kept hidden beneath a thin veneer of respectability.

You can visit Lou's Seattle, thanks to the underground tours begun in 1967 by journalist and self-made historian Bill Speidal. The professional guides tell the 'other' story with all the skills of contemporary storytellers, which many of them are.

The tour guides, however, don't mention another hidden people, for Seattle was also built on the ancestral land of the Duwamish, *Dxʷdəwʔabš* in the Lushootseed language, the 'People of the Inside'. Their land stretched along the salmon-rich valley that bears their name, and their lives revolved around the fish weirs made of willow and stone that diverted and trapped the Pacific salmon as they returned in the summer to spawn. Dried fish kept the people through the long, wet winters and the Duwamish referred to the salmon as friends.

Back in the spring of 2019, I spent a day in the company of Duwamish historian Jay Miller and Mary Lynne Evans of the Puget Sound Welsh Association. We walked up Granny's Hill, named after the tribe's first ancestor, surrounded now by industrial estates, suburban housing and a native shanty street. We climbed to the accompaniment of gunfire from the nearby Seattle Police shooting range, while Jay told a story that had been written down in 1916 by elders Big John (Green River), Charles Sotaiakum (Duwamish), Ann Jack (Green River), Major Hamilton (Duwamish), Sampson and Lucy (Green River and Lake Washington), Dan Silelus (Lake Washington), and Joe Young (Puyallup).

Mountain Beaver lived on top of the hill with her Granny, overlooking two villages on either side of the Duwamish River. North Wind lived in one and South Wind in the other, and both were in love with Mountain Beaver. She was attracted to the warmth of South Wind. In summer they caught salmon together by the fishing weir, and soon she carried his child. When autumn came, North Wind and his ice people crossed the river at the fishing weir, where they killed South Wind, captured Mountain Beaver and her unborn child and built an ice dam over the river to keep the salmon away and starve the southern people.

Mountain Beaver's child was raised as the son of North Wind, and they named him Storm Wind. He grew to resemble his real father, South Wind, and one day Storm Wind was out hunting when he came to Granny's Hill. He climbed to the summit, where he saw a ramshackle old house with crows circling around. He went inside and there was an old woman weaving baskets, huddled in a blanket by a cold, old fire, with her face covered in the frozen tears she had cried every day since her granddaughter had been taken.

Granny recognised Storm Wind as her grandson and sat him down by the fire and told the story of how North Wind had imprisoned her on the hill with crows to guard her so Mountain Beaver would never see her. And Storm Wind understood his real father was South Wind.

Storm Wind built a fire to warm his grandmother, washed the ice-tears from her face and stayed with her through the winter while she told him the stories of the tribe. When spring came, he was strong and wise enough to confront his stepfather.

Storm Wind uprooted trees and threw them from the hillside into the Duwamish River, where they broke the ice that blocked the fish weir. As the water flowed, he walked down the hill to the river, lifted a tree trunk as if it was a feather and told the people he had come to avenge his real father.

When North Wind heard this, he sent his sister to fetch Storm Wind. She dressed in her finest ice jewellery and told Storm Wind her brother wished to see him, but he melted her jewellery and told her that North Wind must come to him.

And so, Storm Wind, true son of South Wind, fought North Wind on the banks of the Duwamish River. Granny heard the sound of the battle below and took two baskets, one with a tight weave filled with water that she sprinkled over the land as fine rain to melt the ice and snow. The other had a loose weave filled with melting ice and snow that she dropped on top of the hill. The water flowed down into the soil and soon the land was cloaked in green.

Spring came, and to the sound of rushing water, Storm Wind defeated North Wind and the salmon returned to the Duwamish River. From that day, North Wind has never felt the warmth of the sun, and each autumn he returns to chase the salmon away, until Storm Wind defeats him in the spring and brings the salmon home, and so the cycle of the seasons was born.

From the top of Granny's Hill, we looked down at the expensive suburban houses climbing up the hillside, contrasting with a few wooden shanties in the valley. The gunfire from the police firing range seemed strangely appropriate, as Jay explained that piece of land was once worked by five brothers who brought 'thunder' to the people. We stopped off at the fishing weir to see a set of sculptures by Coast Salish artist Susan Point that tell the story of the battle between North Wind and South Wind.

In the afternoon, Jay took us to the Duwamish longhouse, built of carved cedar posts and beams by *potlatch* architects to traditional Salish designs. It stands on a small piece of repurchased ancestral land surrounded by industrial units that cover the old settlement of Ha-AH-Poos. It opened in 2009 as a cultural centre and meeting place for the 500 official tribal members, and stands in stark contrast to the monolithic red and gold Emerald Queen Casino built recently for the neighbouring Puyallup tribe in Tacoma, which has a 2,000-seat event space, two casinos, 200 slot machines, five restaurants, sports bars and a multi-storey car park big enough to fit a town of longhouses.

We met Chairwoman Cecile Hansen, great-great-great-grand-niece of Si'áb Si'ahl, Chief Seattle, who had signed the treaty of Port Elliott in 1854 that tricked him into giving away 54,700 acres of Duwamish land to the settlers, in exchange for their own reservation. He was double crossed, the Duwamish received no land, were burned out of their homes and even today have neither federal nor tribal recognition.

Officially, the Duwamish don't exist. They are the ultimate hidden people.

As Cecile Hansen has repeated for almost fifty years, to anyone with ears to listen and eyes to see:

'We're still here.'

32

The Crow and the Canary:
Part Two

CYMRU, WALES

(Continued from p.21)

I n September 1944, Dylan the changeling child, together with the golden-haired Princess Caitlin and their two young children, Llewelyn and Aeronwy, settled into a ramshackle fairy-tale cottage on the clifftop overlooking Cardigan Bay, next to the mansion and church at Llanina and a sea full of frolicking, drunken mermaids.

Well, it was more of a bungalow built of paper-thin walls and asbestos with a *tŷ bach*, an outside loo, where Dylan hid to avoid paying the £1 a week rent. He was often seen wheeling Aeronwy's pram full of beer bottles along the beach, where he sat under the overhanging wood sipping a milk stout. The good Ceredigion folk soon spotted his little ways.

Dylan was inspired here. He heard the voices of the old sea captains speaking to their drowned lovers. He imagined coffins washed up on the beach after storms from the graveyard beneath the sea. He knew the tale of how mermaids rescued the shipwrecked Saxon King Ina, who thanked them by naming the church after himself, Llan Ina. He heard these stories from his neighbour in Sketty, Myra Evans, who was born in Ceinewydd, a short walk away along the clifftop.

Myra, her mischievous son Aneurin and youngest daughter Iola were settling into their blue bungalow in Gilfachreda, just down the lane from Dylan. Her husband Evan had died, her four other children had flown the nest, and Myra was writing, drawing, making beaver hats and teaching Welsh, while Aneurin was working at nearby Aberporth Airbase. He was often seen walking home after a night out with Dylan in the Black Lion in Ceinewydd, a giant of a man wearing a flowery shirt and sombrero, cars swerving round him, unable to offer a lift because he was too big to fit through the doors. The locals nicknamed him 'King Kong'.

One evening, Myra, dressed in the apron she always wore, was cooking mackerel in a griddle pan over the hob, prodding at it with a fork in either hand. Iola sat at the table wrapped in a blanket, clutching a mug of cocoa to warm herself after being challenged by the boys to pole vault the stream. Aneurin sat next to her looking mountainous. A knock at the door was followed by a voice calling out in a deep, honeyed Swansea accent. Without looking up, Myra replied, '*Yn y gegin*, Dylan, *dewch i mewn.*'

A pram containing a sleeping golden-haired baby girl and a bottle of beer appeared in the doorway, followed by a slight, asthmatic, baggy-trousered man, curly hair turning blond to ash brown, and autumn eyes that almost popped out of his head. Myra sat him down at the head of the table, ladled out a bowl of thin *cawl* and he ate hungrily.

In between mouthfuls, he said it was a madhouse at home, with Caitlin and the kids shrieking at each other, so he'd decided to rent the apple-house at Plas Llanina as a writing shed. He had an idea for a story about a town that was certified mad by a government inspector, though the inhabitants preferred their madness to the sanity of the normal world.

And here he was, near Ceinewydd, home to thirty-five retired, ocean-voyaging sea captains, with a Captain Cat in every window of Cockle Row, Phoebe Evans was a real-life Polly Garter, and there was Willy Nilly, Mary Ann, the Donkey Man and all the never-to-be-forgotten people of his imagination. Myra knew them all. She filled sketchbooks with portraits of them, but never told anyone. Only Dr Jones had seen them after she accidentally dropped a sketchbook in his surgery and he politely picked it up for her, flicked through the pages and smiled wryly.

Dylan told Myra he wanted to ask her something. She gave him a thought-as-much glance and placed a mackerel fillet in front of him. He asked her to teach Welsh to his son Llewelyn. Maybe him, too? He would pay, of course.

Myra pokered the fire. Iola stared from beneath her fringe of black hair. Aneurin said he had to see a man about a dog and would be in the Black Lion later for a pint. Myra placed her hand on Dylan's arm and told him he could write as sweetly as a canary could sing, but she was an old crow now, the wrong side of 60, grieving for her Evan and with young Iola to look after.

Dylan nodded, sucked the last mackerel from the bones and asked her to tell him a story, the one about the Llanina mermaid. Myra picked up her thread work and began to stitch, and as her fingers danced to the rhythm of her words, she nodded towards the window and began.

☙✦❧

The sea out there in Cardigan Bay was once a fabled land of forests, lakes and rivers, and out there was a smallholding called Tangeulan, home to Nidan, a widow woman, and her son, Rhysyn. He was a fisherman, while his mother salted and dried the herring and mended the nets after the seals bit holes in them. Rhysyn had dark curling hair, like so many of the boys in the west, and he was engaged to Lowri, with her hair of spun gold, who had migrated from the south to work as a maid at the big house, Plas Llanina. They were to be wed at the church on the next *Gŵyl Mabsant*, Saints Day.

One evening, when the sky above Cardigan Bay was the colour of primroses, violets and campion, Rhysyn was hauling in his golden-gutted nets, singing Lowri's song about a mermaid with spun gold hair, when he saw, sat on the rocks at Carreg Ina, combing her red seaweedy hair, a mermaid. The evening sun cast shadows below her ribs, and her tail was covered in barnacles and limpets. She wasn't at all like the mermaids in the picture books.

'Beautiful evening?' he called.

The mermaid turned, and answered in Welsh, 'That song about the mermaid with spun gold hair. Teach me that song, fisherman.'

Rhysyn rowed closer. 'I will. What's your name?'

'Morwen, daughter of Nefus, King of the Deeps.'

Rhysyn sang his song, Morwen flushed, and as she vanished beneath the water, she said, 'I will be here every evening until I sing as sweetly as you.'

Rhysyn was strangely attracted to this wild fish-girl, so the following evening he returned to Carreg Ina, and every evening until Morwen could sing his song.

She was entranced by him and invited him to live in her land below the waves, where they would swim together arm in arm. Rhysyn watched as a small crab crawled through her hair and a periwinkle moved slowly and unnervingly along her tail. He told her he was to wed Lowri, maid of Plas Llanina.

Morwen twisted her red hair between her fingers, raised her tail in the air and thrashed it against the water, time after time, until the turbulence of rejection receded. 'Fisherman, my father is the sea, and he will be angry,' and she vanished beneath the water.

Rhysyn was shaken. He went home and refused to go fishing. Nidan noticed the change in her son and called Lowri, who shed a tear, for men always pulled her to them, then tossed her away like a plaything.

The day of the wedding dawned bright and clear and Rhysyn sat on the shore, feeling his golden-gutted nets between his fingers, when Morwen appeared, head and shoulders above the water. 'Rhysyn, son of Nidan, if you go to Llanina Church, my father will take your mother's house at Tangeulan.' And she slipped beneath the waves.

Nidan dragged Rhysyn to the church as the skies turned grey, and he saw Lowri standing by the altar looking so desirable in her white dress and he knew she was the only woman he would ever truly love.

A great storm gathered and the sea churned. It covered the house at Tangeulan, rushed in through the doors of the church and Rhysyn was swept out to sea. As he sank into the depths, he saw red, tangled, seaweedy hair and felt arms around him, his two legs became one and he swam like a fish.

The sea took the church, the coastal farms, their chickens and sheep, and dolphins swim where people once walked. And when the evening sky is painted with primrose, campion and violets, listen and you may hear church bells from the lost land beneath the sea, ringing the marriage of Rhysyn and Morwen.

Dylan took out a notebook and wrote, 'The Ballad of the Long-legg'd Bait'.

Myra opened a sketchbook, drew Dylan, and wrote, '*Gofynnodd i mi ddysgu Cymraeg iddo!*' ('He asked me to teach him Welsh!')

Aeronwy stirred in her pram, Dylan put down his pen, laughed at Myra's drawing of him with a cigarette dangling from his lips, and said, 'Time I returned to my lost land under the sea.'

Myra looked drained, as if all the stories she ever knew had left her. Iola asked her mother why she had turned down the famous Mr Dylan. Myra explained that he was in debt to her friends, owed money to the traders and borrowed to buy a round of drinks. He would never have paid.

Dylan was the hero with a thousand faces, trickster and tricked, lover and lovelorn, mermaid and fisherman, changeling and human child, crow and canary. Shortly before he left for his final trip to the States in 1953, Oxford University Press invited him to edit a collection of *Welsh Fairy Tales and Legends*. Had he lived, he may have written his own mythology.

Myra died in Aberystwyth in 1972 aged 89, having lived half a century longer than Dylan. She left a priceless gift of fairy tales, true tales, songs and recipes, and is buried with her husband and son in the non-denominational cemetery on the hill outside Ceinewydd, a few fields away from the Llwynwermwnt Farmhouse and the changeling child, where our story began.

Epilogue
Plant Rhys Ddwfn

BAE CEREDIGION, FARRAIGE NA HÉIREANN, IRISH SEA

This book ends as it began, with a small boy standing on the stone walls of the Giants' Town on Tre-r Ceiri, squinting through the mist to see faraway countries, submerged lands and forgotten utopias.

The sea out there in Cardigan Bay, from Pen Llŷn in the north to Cemaes in the south, was once a land of forests, lakes and rivers. The people who lived there were small and fair, they cared for the plants and animals, took only as much food as they needed, always left an offering in exchange and never once believed they owned the land. They were known as *Plant Rhys Ddwfn*, the Children of Rhys the Deep.

Not deep below the sea – Rhys was a thinker, a philosopher. He hid the land from the prying eyes of the mainlanders by planting a hedge of herbs the length of what is now the Welsh coast. Only if you stood on the one small patch of this herb that grew on a mountain would you see Rhys's land, and if you stepped away you would forget how to see it again. As no one on the mainland knew where the patch of herbs was, they never saw the Welsh Utopia. All they saw was rain.

The Rhysians loved each other. They had children, their numbers grew, they felled the forests for timber to build homes and fished the rivers and lakes to feed their hunger. The mainlanders heard the distant sound of the rumbling of bellies and mistook it for the anger of the gods.

The Rhysians took to craftwork. They made wooden bowls and cast-iron cauldrons and traded by sea like the Phoenicians before them. They visited the market at Aberteifi, but when the traders saw them coming, prices went up. The poor folk said they were friends of Phil Siôn Hywel the farmer, not Dafydd the labourer.

They traded with Gruffydd ap Einion, a free-thinking radical who dreamed of a better world, whose corn was always fresh and

prices fair. As the years passed, the Rhysians gifted Gruffydd by taking him to the clump of herbs on the mountain, where he saw all the knowledge and wisdom in the world, archived in forests and libraries. Preachers and politicians were few. Sheep were plentiful. It was the utopia he had always dreamed of.

Gruffydd asked how they kept themselves safe, and they explained that Rhys's hedge of herbs hid them behind a veil of watery mist. All they had to remind them of the mainland was a curious drawing of a creature with horns, a bosom of snakes, the legs of an ass, holding a great knife, with bodies lying all around. No one wished to meet that creature.

When Gruffydd stepped away from the patch of herbs, he forgot how to see Rhys's land, although it remained in his dreams and memories until his hair turned to snow and he passed over to the otherworld. The Rhysians never returned to Aberteifi.

Yet Rhys's utopia is still there. Look beyond the reflections in the windows of the little train that trundles along the Cambrian coast. It's not a lost land submerged beneath the sea, but a philosophy of equality, justice and kindness.

In my childhood imagination, that one patch of herbs grew on Tre'r Ceiri, by the stone roundhouses of the Giants' Town, where I squinted through the mist at utopia. Oh, and 'Plant Rhys Ddwfn' is colloquial Welsh for those who lived here before, the marginalised, the dispossessed, the otherworldly, the hidden people:

Y Tylwyth teg.

Bibliography

General

Ashliman, D.L., *Fairy Lore: A Handbook* (Westport: Connecticut, 2006).

Briggs K.M., *The Fairies in Tradition and Literature* (London: Routledge, 1967).

Carter, Angela, *Strange Things Sometimes Still Happen: Fairy Tales from Around the World* (Boston: Faber & Faber, 1993).

Johnson, Donald S., *Phantom Islands of the Atlantic, The Legends of Seven Lands that Never Were* (New York: Walker & Co., 1996).

Opie, Iona and Peter, *The Classic Fairy Tales* (Oxford University Press, 1974).

Packer, Alison, Bedoe, Stella and Lianne Jarrett, *Fairies in Legend and the Arts* (London: David & Charles, 1980).

Purkiss, Diane, *Troublesome Things: A History of Fairies and Fairy Stories* (London: Penguin, 2000).

Stevenson, Peter, *The Moon-Eyed People: Folk Tales from Welsh America* (Stroud: History Press, 2019).

Tatar, Maria, *The Fairest of Them All: and 21 Tales of Mothers and Daughters* (Harvard University Press, 2020).

Warner, Marina, *No Go the Bogeyman* (London: Chatto & Windus, 1998).

Young, Simon, and Ceri Houlbook (eds), *Magical Folk: British and Irish Fairies, 500 AD to the Present* (London: Gibson Square, 2018).

Zipes, Jack, *Fairy Tales and the Art of Subversion* (New York: Methuen, 1983).

Websites

Andonov, Viktor, www.worldoftales.com/folktales.html

Ashliman, D.L., www.pitt.edu/~dash/folktexts.html

Folklore Thursday, folklorethursday.com

Folklore Society, folklore-society.com

Heiner, Heidi Anne, www.surlalunefairytales.com

Hulse, Ty, zeluna.net

Oral Tradition, journal.oraltradition.org

Taletellerin taletellerin.wordpress.com

Young, Simon www.fairyist.com/survey

Chapters

The Crow and the Canary, Part 1

Billings, Iola, 'Oral Family Stories'.

Evans, Myra, *Casgliad o Chwedlau Newydd* (Aberystwyth: Cambrian News, 1926).

Evans, Myra, private unpublished papers.

Gwyndaf, Robin, Recordings and papers in St Fagan's.

Passmore, S.C., *Farmers and Figureheads: The Port of New Quay and its Hinterland* (Dyfed County Council, 1992).

Stevenson, Peter, *Dylan Thomas* (Stroud: Pitkin, 2014).

Stevenson, Peter, *Ceredigion Folk Tales* (Stroud: History Press, 2014).

Thomas, David N., *Dylan Thomas: A Farm, Two Mansions, and a Bungalow* (Bridgend: Seren, 2009).

Thanks to Iola Billings, Ceri Owen-Jones, Elsa Davies, Jake Whittaker, Owen Shiers, Robin Gwyndaf, Sue Passmore, and Mary Jane Stephenson.

The Silkie Painter

Campbell, David, and Duncan Williamson, *A Traveller in Two Worlds, Volume One: The Early Life of Scotland's Wandering Bard* (Edinburgh: Luath, 2011).

Campbell, David, and Duncan Williamson, *A Traveller in Two Worlds, Volume Two: The Tinker and the Student* (Edinburgh: Luath, 2011).

MacDougall, Rev. James, and Rev. George Calder (eds), *Folk Tales and Fairy Lore in Gaelic and English* (Edinburgh: John Grant, 1910).

MacGregor, Alasdair Alpin, *The Peat-Fire Flame, Folk-Tales and Traditions of the Highlands & Islands* (Edinburgh: Moray Press, 1937).

Williamson, Duncan, *Tales of the Seal People* (Northampton Ma: Interlink Books, 1992).

Thanks to the Institute for Dialect and Folklife Studies.

Boggart Hole Clough

Bamford, Samuel, *Passages in the Life of a Radical*, Vols 1 & 2 (Manchester, 1839–44).

Houlbrook, Ceri, 'The Suburban Boggart: Folklore of an Inner-City Park' in *Gramarye: The Journal of the Sussex Centre for Folklore, Fairy Tales and Fantasy*, Vol. 11 (University of Chichester, May 2017).

Roby, John, *Traditions of Lancashire* (London: Longman Rees, 1829).

Stevenson, Peter, *Welsh Folk Tales* (Stroud: History Press, 2017).

Young, Simon, *Boggart Dialect Literature and a Handlist of Boggart Works* (Centre for English Traditional Heritage / Umbra Institute).

The Glashtyn

Angwin, Fiona, *Manx Folk Tales* (Stroud: History Press, 2015).

Broome, Dora, *Fairy Tales from the Isle of Man* (London: Penguin, 1951) pp.48–53.

Moore, A.W., *Folklore of the Isle of Man* (Isle of Man: Brown and Son, 1891).

Morrison, Sophia, *Manx Fairy Tales* (London: David Nutt, 1911) pp.75–78.

Thanks to Felix Parker-Price and Cat Weatherill.

The Sceach and the Seanchaí

Lenihan, Eddie, with Carolyn Eve Green, *Meeting the Other Crowd: The Fairy Stories of Hidden Ireland* (Dublin: Gill Books, 2003).

Lally, Steve, and Paula Flynn Lally, *Irish Gothic: Fairy Stories from Ireland's 32 Counties* (Cheltenham: History Press, 2019).

The Burren and Beyond: theburrenandbeyond.com

Thanks to Eddie Lenihan.

The Stonewaller and the Korrigan

Le Braz, Anatole (trans. by Derek Bryce from the original French of Anatole Le Braz), *Celtic Legends of the Beyond* (Lampeter: Llanerch, 1986).

Carrington, Dorothy, *The Dream-Hunters of Corsica* (London: Weidenfeld & Nicholson, 1995).

Dixon, Marjorie, *Breton Fairy Tales* (London: Gollancz 1971) pp.86–97.

Luzel, F.M. (trans. by Derek Bryce), *Celtic Folk-Tales from Armorica* (Lampeter: Llanerch, 1985).

Souvestre, Émile, *Le Foyer Breton / The Breton Hearth* (W. Coquebert, 1844).

Thanks to Samuel Allo, Derek Bryce and Valériane Leblond.

Schneeweißen und Rosenroot

Forsyth, Kate, *The Secret History of the Grimm Fairy Tales* (Folklore Thursday, 2017): folklorethursday.com/folktales/secret-history-grimm-fairy-tales

Heiner, Heidi Anne, *Snow White & Rose Red – Annotated Tale*: https://www.surlalunefairytales.com/s-z/snow-white-red-rose/snow-white-red-rose-annotations.html

Ness, Mari, *Creating a Tale of Sister-Hood: Snow-White and Rose-Red*: www.tor.com/2018/01/25/creating-a-tale-of-sisterhood-snow-white-and-rose-red/ (Tor.com, 2018).

Zipes, Jack (ed.), *The Complete First Edition: The Original Folk & Fairy Tales of the Brothers Grimm* (New Jersey: Princeton University Press 2014) pp.132–33.

A Tale of Tales

Basile, Giambattista, *The Tale of Tales, or Entertainment for Little Ones / Lo cunto de li cunti overo lo trattenemiento de peccerille*, also known as *Il Pentamerone*, two volumes (Naples, Italy, 1634 and 1636).

Crane, Thomas Frederick and Jack Zipes (eds), *Italian Popular Tales* (Oxford University Press, 2003).

Garrone, Matteo (dir.), *Lo Cunto de li Cunti / The Tale of Tales* (2015).

Rohrwacher, Alice (dir.), *Lazzaro Felice / Happy as Lazzaro* (2018).

Sjökungen and the Troll Artist

Agrenius, Helen, *The Artist John Bauer and His World* (Jonkopping County Museum, 1996).

Nyblom, Helena, and John Bauer, *Agneta och Sjökungen: Bland tomtar och troll* (Åhlén & Åkerlund, 1910).

Blecher, Lone Thygesen, and George Blecher, *Swedish Folktales and Legends* (Minneapolis: University of Minnesota Press, 1993).

Booss, Claire (ed.), *Scandinavian Folk and Fairy Tales* (New York: Avenal Books, 1984).

Trolls

Asbjørnsen, Peter Christen, and Jørgen Moe (trans. by George Webbe Dasent), *Norske Folkeeventyr / Norwegian Folktales: Popular Tales From the Norse* (Edinburgh: David Douglass, Third Edition, 1888).

Gaiman, Neil, *On the Good Kind of Trolls* (Literary Hub, 2019): lithub.com/neil-gaiman-on-the-good-kind-of-trolls

Lindow, John, *Trolls, an Unnatural History* (London: Reaktion Books, 2014).

Nunnally, Tiina, *The Complete and Original Norwegian Folktales of Asbjørnsen and Moe* (University of Minnesota Press, 2019).

Ulda Girl and Sámi Boy

Cocq, Coppélie, *Revoicing Sámi Narratives: North Sámi Storytelling at the Turn of the 20th Century* (Umeå University, 2008).

Hatt, Emilie Demant (trans. by Barbara Sjoholm), *By the Fire, Sámi Folktales and Legends* (University of Minnesota Press, 2019).

Sjoholm, Barbara, *Black Fox: A Life of Emilie Demant Hatt, Artist and Ethnographer* (Madison: Univ. of Wisconsin Press, 2017).

Turi, Johan (trans. by Thomas A. DuBois), *An Account of the Sámi* (Nordic Studies Press, 2011).

Huldufólk and the Icelandic Bank Crash

Árnason, Jon, *Íslenzkar Þjóðsögur og Æfintýri* (Leipzig: J.C. Hinrichs, 1862).

Árnason, Jón (trans. by George E.J. Powell and Eiríkur Magnússon), *Icelandic Legends* (London: Richard Bentley, 1864), pp.19–21.

Hall, Alaric, 'Why Aren't There Any Elves in Hellisgerdi Anymore? Elves and the 2008 Icelandic Financial Crisis' (working paper, 2014): www.alarichall.org.uk

Kyzer, Larissa, *Hidden People Folktales* (The Reykjavik Grapevine, 2014).

Simpson, Jacqueline, *Icelandic Folktales & Legends* (Stroud: History Press, new ed. 2004).

Otesánek and the Jeziňka Girls Who Steal Eyes

Erben, Karel Jaromir, *Sto prostonárodních pohádek a pověstí slovanských v nářečích původních / One Hundred Slavic Folk Tales and Legends in Original Dialects* (Prague, 1865).

Erben, Karel Jaromir (trans. by Marcela Sulak), *A Bouquet: Of Czech Fairytales* (Prague, Twisted Spoon, 2012).

Němcová, Božena, *The Disobedient Kids and Other Czecho-Slovak Fairy Tales* (Prague: B. Kočí, 1921).

Švankmejer, Jan, and Eva Švankmajerová, *Otesánek / Little Otik* (Czech Republic, 2000).

Thanks to Veronika Derkova.

Nita and the Vampir

Constantinescu, Dr Barbu, *Probe de Limba si Literatura Taganilor din România* (Bucharest, 1878).

Druts, Yefim, and Alexei Gessler (trans. by James Riordan), *Russian Gypsy Tales* (Edinburgh: Canongate, 1986).

Groome, Francis Hindes, *Gypsy Folk Tales* (London: Hurst and Blackett Limited, 1899).

Jarman, Eldra and AOH Jarman, *Y Sipsiwn Cymraeg* (Cardiff: University of Wales, 1979).

Rotaru, Julieta, 'Barbu Constantinescu: The First Romanian Scholar of Romani Studies' in *Continuing Journal of the Gypsy Lore Society* (2018).

Thanks to all the Welsh Romany people, the Roberts family, John Roberts Project and Harriet Earis.

The Copper Man

Lintrop, Aado, 'On the Udmurt Water Spirit and the Formation of the Concept 'Holy' Among Permian Peoples' in *Folklore*, Vol. 26 (2004): www.folklore.ee/folklore/vol26/lintrop.pdf

Shushakova, Galina, 'The Idea of Earthly and Unearthly Worlds in the Udmurt Fairy-tales' in *Folk Belief Today* (Tartu, 1995), pp.442–45.

Vereshchagin, Grigory Egorovich, *Votyaki Sosnovsky Krai* (Izhevsk: UIIAL Ural Branch of the Russian Academy of Sciences, six vols, 1995, first published 1884).

Vladykina, Tat'Yana, 'The Bee in Udmurt Folklore and Mytho-Ritual Practice' in *АЛЬМАНАХ*, Vol. 17. No. 4 (2016), p.64.

The Girl Who Became a Boy

Elsie, Robert, *Albanian Folktales and Legends: Selected and Translated from the Albanian*, Vol. 2 (Create Space, 3rd ed., 2015).

Jones, Rhodri, and Neil Olsen, *Albania* (Oxfam, 2000).

Young, Antonia, *Women Who Become Men: Albanian Sworn Virgins* (London: Berg, 2001).

Dozon, Auguste, *Manuel de la langue chkipe ou albanaise par consul de France: Grammaire, vocabulaire, chrestomathie* (Paris: Ernest Leroux, 1879).

Tanner, Marcus, *Albania's Mountain Queen: Edith Durham and the Balkans* (I.B. Taurus, 2014).

Thanks to Jo Blake Cave.

The Hidden People of Anatolia

Barnham, Henry D. (trans.), *Tales of Nasr-ed-din Khoja* (London: Nisbet & Co., 1923).

Kúnos, Ignácz, *Turkish Fairy Tales and Folk Tales – Collected by D. Ignácz Kúnos*, translated from the Hungarian version by R. Nisbet Bain (London: Lawrence & Bullen, 1896).

Walker, Barbara K., *Turkish Folk-Tales* (Oxford University Press, 1988), pp.62–66.

Thanks to Sitki Tellioglu.

The Bewitched Camel

Galland, Antoine, 'Prince Ahmed and the Fairy Pari-Banou', in Jack Zipes, *Spells of Enchantment* (New York: Penguin, 1991), pp.122–59.

Risha, Zulaikha Abu, and Serene Huleileh (trans.), *Timeless Tales Told by Syrian Refugees* (Stockholm: Cultural Heritage without Borders, 2015).

Tahlan, Samir, *Folktales from Syria* (Austin: University of Texas, 2004).

Reiniger, Lotte (dir.), *Die Abenteuer des Prinzen Achmed | The Adventures of Prince Achmed* (Germany, 1926).

Warner, Marina, *Stranger Magic, Charmed States and the Arabian Nights* (London: Chatto & Windus, 2011).

Thanks to Mohamad Karkoubi and family for the inspiration.

A Tale from the Tamarind Tree

Ames, David W., 'The Dual Function of the "Little People" of the Forest in the Lives of the Wolof' in *The Journal of American Folklore*, 279, 23 (1958).

Senghor, Leopold Sédar, Preface by Amadou Koumba to Birago Diop, in Diop, Birago, *The New Tales of Amadou Koumba* (Paris: African Presence, 1958).

Diop, Birago, *Les Contes d'Amadou-Koumba* (Paris: Présence Afraicaine, 1947).

Mercier, Roger, and M. and S. Battestini, *Birago Diop, Senegalese Writer* (Paris: F. Nathan, 1964).

The Hare and the Tortoise

Baissac, Charles, *Les Littératures Populaires de Toutes les Nations – Le Folk-lore de l'île Maurice* (Paris: 1888).
Ramsurrun, Pahlad, *Folk Tales of Mauritius* (New Delhi: Star Publishers, 2014).
Romero-Frias, Xavier, *Folk Tales of the Maldives* (Copenhagen: Nordic Institute of Asian Studies, 2012).
November, Kiat, 'The Hare and the Tortoise Down by the King's Pond: A Tale of Four Translations' in *Meta*, Vol. 52, Issue 2, June 2007, pp.194–201 (Les Presses de l'Université de Montréal).
Zephaniah, Benjamin, 'Britain's Shameful Treatment of Chagos Islanders Must End', *Guardian*, 16 January 2018.

Thanks to Josian Fauzou.

Weretiger

Brighenti, Francesco, 'Traditional Beliefs About Weretigers Among the Garos of Maghalaya (India)' in *eTropic*, 16.1, p.96 (2017).
Jenkins, Nigel, *Gwalia in Khasia* (Gomer: Llandysul, 1995).
Kharmawphlang, Desmond, 'In Search of Tigermen: The Weretiger Tradition of the Khasis' in *India International Centre Quarterly*, Vol. 27, No. 4/Vol. 28, No. 1, pp.160–76 (2000/2001).
Rafy, Mrs, *Folk-Tales of the Khasis* (London: MacMillan, 1920).
Suting, Willie Gordon, 'Tiger Tales in Khasi Clans' in *The Shillong Times*, 25 July 2018.

Yakshi

Maddy, *The Bewitching Yakshi* (2010): https://maddy06.blogspot.com/2010/02/bewitching-yakshi.html
Menon, I.K.K., *Folk Tales of Kerala* (Publications Division, Ministry of Information & Broadcasting, Govt of India, 1995) pp.90–91.
Narayan, T.C., Lore and Legends of Kerala: Selections from Kottarathil Sankunni's Aithihyamala (Oxford University Press, 2010).
Pattanaik, Devdutt, *The Yakshi's Solicitation* (20 April, 2015): https://devdutt.com/articles/the-yakshis-solicitation/
Menon, Anasuva, *The Yakshi Who Ended a War and Other Stories* (Bluepea, July 2020).

The Fox and the Ghost

Chan, Leo Tak-hung, *The Discourse on Foxes and Ghosts: Ji Yun and Eighteenth-Century Literati Storytelling* (Honolulu: University of Hawai-i, 1998).
Chinese Storytelling: www.shuoshu.org/Chinese_Storytelling/index.shtml
Pu Songling (trans. by John Minford), *Strange Stories from a Chinese Studio* (London: Penguin, 2006).
Watters, Thomas, 'Chinese Fox-Myths' in *Journal of the North-China Branch of the Royal Asiatic Society*, VIII (1874).
Xianyi, Yang (trans.), *Stories About Not Being Afraid of Ghosts* (Foreign Languages Press, 1961).

Thanks to Veronika Derkova.

Yōkai

Codrescu, Andrei (ed.), *Japanese Tales of Lafcadio Hearn* (Princeton University Press, 2019).

Foster, Michael Dylan, *The Book of Yōkai:, Mysterious Creatures of Japanese Folklore* (Oakland: University of California Press, 2015).

Mayazaki, Hayao (dir.), *Princess Mononoke* (Studio Ghibli, 1997).

Hearn, Lafcadio (trans.), *Japanese Fairy Tales: Chin Chin Kobakama* (Tokyo: T. Hasegawa, 1903).

Thanks to Tom Stevenson and Veronika Derkova.

Patupaiarehe

Cowan, James, *Fairy Folk Tales of the Māori* (Auckland: Whitcombe & Tombs, 1925).

Various authors, *Parihaka* (National Library of New Zealand): natlib.govt.nz/schools/topics/5b99d6908d2a4e164e3f707e/parihaka

Waititi, Taika (dir.), *Boy* (2010).

Thanks to Moira Wairama, Tony Hopkins, Judith Frost-Evans, Caroline Welkin, Ralph Johnson, Linda Hansen and Greg Cameron.

River Mumma

Arnott, Paul, *Windrush: A Ship Through Time* (Stroud: History Press, 2019).

Evans, Chris, *Slave Wales: The Welsh and Atlantic Slavery 1600–1850* (Cardiff: University of Wales, 2010).

Hurston, Zora Neale, *Tell My Horse: Voodoo and Life in Haiti and Jamaica* (Philadelphia: Lippincott, 1938).

'Obara Meji', 'Elvis and de River Mumma' (2 March 2015): www.embracingspirituality.com/

'The Girl from Lethe', 'Supernatural Stories, Part 1: Our Rivah Mumma' (27 September 2017): thegirlfromlethe.wordpress.com

The People Who Could Fly

Chater, Kathleen, *Henry Box Brown: from Slavery to Showbusiness* (Jefferson NC: McFarland, 2020).

Cutter, Martha J., 'Will the Real Henry "Box" Brown Please Stand Up' in *Common Place*, 16.1, Fall 2015).

Georgia Writers' Project, *Drums and Shadows: Survival Studies Among the Georgia Coastal Negroes* (Athens: University of Georgia Press, 1940).

Jones Jr, Charles Colcock, *Gullah Folktales from the Georgia Coast* (University of Georgia, 2000, first printed 1888).

Young, Jason R., 'All God's Children had Wings: The Flying African in History, Literature, and Lore' in *Journal of Africana Religions*, Vol. 5, No.1 (Penn State University Press: 2017), pp.50–70.

Thanks to Phil Okwedy.

The Woman Who Fell in Love With a Pumpkin

Arner, Robert D., 'The Story of Hannah Duston: Cotton Mather to Thoreau' in *American Transcendental Quarterly*, 18, (1973) pp.19–23.

Clapp, John Irving, *A Tale of Two Cabins: Comparative Stories of Thoreau's Cabin, Nature, and Life* (Amherst: Levellers Press, 2015).

Diwasa, Tilasi, *Folk Tales from Nepal* (New Delhi: Publications Division, Ministry of Information and Broadcasting, Govt. of India, 2003).

Scanlon, Laura Wolff, 'A Bhutanese Folktale Becomes a Children's Book in New Hampshire' in *Humanities*, Vol. 39, No.1 (Winter 2018).

Speare, Eva A., *New Hampshire Folk tales* (Canaan NH: Phoenix, 7th ed 1974, 1st ed. 1945) p.193.

Tiwari, Hari, and Dai Rai, Terry Farish, Narad Adhikari, *The Story of a Pumpkin* (Concord: New Hampshire Humanities Council, 2013).

Thanks to Alison and Lisa Matthews and John Clapp.

Appalachian Mister Fox

Chase, Richard, *American Folk Tales and Songs* (New York: Signet, 1956), pp.31–42.

Musick, Ruth Ann, *Green Hills of Magic: West Virginia Folk Tales from Europe* (Lexington, University of Kentucky, 1970).

Musick, Ruth Ann (ed.), *Mountain Mother Goose: Child Lore of West Virginia* (Fairmont State University Press, 2013).

Tan, Caitlin, 'Art Exhibit Explores Appalachia's Connection to Wales' (West Virginia Public Broadcasting, 2019): www.wvpublic.org/post/art-exhibit-explores-appalachias-connection-wales#stream/0

Thanks to Judi Tarowsky, Granny Sue, Alan Hoal, Jamie Lester, Caitlin Tan, Nick Stamm, Alison and Ed Anderson, Mark Kemp and all the Morgantown Kemps.

Cherokee Little People

Conley, Robert, Cherokee Medicine Man: The Life and Work of a Modern-Day Healer (Norman: University of Oklahoma 2005), pp.93–94.

Lombardi, Betty J., 'Comments on the Little People: Stories Collected from the Cherokee Indians of Northeast Oklahoma' in *Mid-American Folklore* (Ozark State Folklore Society, 1984).

Lossiah, Lynn, *Cherokee Little People: The Secrets and Mysteries of the Yunwi Tsunsdi* (Cherokee Publications, 1998).

Mooney, James, *Myths of the Cherokee* (Washington: US Bureau of American Ethnology, 1902).

Reed, Jeannie, *Stories of the Yunwi Tsunsdi: The Cherokee Little People* (Cullowhee: Western Carolina University, 1991).

Thanks to Tony Hopkins.

We're Still Here

Anon., 'Sin City: A Red Light History of Seattle' (*Seattle Met*, February 2010).

Duwamish Tribe, website www.duwamishtribe.org

Miller, Jay, *Salmon, the Lifegiving Gift* (University of Washington Digital Collections).

Speidel, Bill, 'The Hostess with the Mostest' in *Sons of the Profits* (Seattle: Nettle Creek, 1967), pp.283–304.

Thanks to Jay Miller, Cecile Hansen and Mary Lynne Evans.

The Crow and the Canary, Part Two

See 'The Crow and the Canary, Part One'.

Epilogue: Plant Rhys Ddwfn

Stevenson, Peter, *Ceredigion Folk Tales* (Stroud: History Press, 2014).